THE TRAVELER

A METAPHYSICAL JOURNEY

Robert D. Andrews

Order this book online at www.trafford.com
or email orders@trafford.com

Most Trafford titles are also available at major online book retailers.

Printed in the United States of America.

ISBN: 978-1-4907-2168-2 (sc)
ISBN: 978-1-4907-2167-5 (e)

Trafford rev. 01/10/2014

www.trafford.com

North America & international
toll-free: 1 888 232 4444 (USA & Canada)
fax: 812 355 4082

CONTENTS

BOOK ONE

DEDICATION

I wish to dedicate this book to the people in my family for their share in my many learnings:

To my wife, JoAnn; my daughter, Robin and her spouse, Chris; my son, Mark, and his wife, Babbette; my stepdaughter, Rachel, and her husband, Peter; my foster son, Mike, and his wife, Cheryl; and my sister, Valerie, and her husband, Andy.

To my grandchildren, Emily, Justin, Nico, and Larissa.
May your journey be filled with pleasure, learning, adventure, and success.

ACKNOWLEDGEMENTS

A special thanks for their important influence goes to:

A Word on Wednesday in Northampton, MA
When Elliot Tarry was the leader

Patricia Lee Lewis
Patchwork Farm Retreat
Encourager of my writing

Janet Sadler
The Springfield Museum, MA
Encourager of my writing

Eric Bascomb
Springfield, MA
Encourager of my writing

Diane Malachowski
A special encourager

Nancy Sicbaldi
My co-editor, arranger, and supporter

JoAnn Andrews
My patient wife and encourager

CHAPTER ONE

....

THE INVITATION

"You travel far to join us in meditation. How long have you been coming to learn? Has it been two years?"

"Almost three," answered David. "I feel calmer and more relaxed. My temper has all but disappeared."

"That is good news to hear. I know three years seems like a long time, yet we spend years in seminary to become a Monk of the Yellow Hat tradition. Meditation becomes a way to open new pathways in our awareness and our ability to use our senses. Many of us feel we can experience additional ways to exist on this plain."

David looked at the monk. "I have been having unusual experiences when I meditate."

"Unusual? Tell me about it." The monk seemed curious.

David sat straight and closed his eyes.

"Sometimes I enter there-after practicing exploring the space between breaths—those sacred moments that reveal answers to questions I sometimes fear to ask.

Yet, when I do, the part of me I like to ignore and the part of me public to myself come together and create awareness—integrating gently sometimes, coming together for the first time, stronger within me, strangers to a part of me—strengths unknown to each other.

I then begin moving between night and day.

It places me in a loving, peaceful place—yet the aliveness of energy touches me, a massage of healing.

It caresses my essential essence—

Nurturing, cuddling, bombarding my senses with pleasure.

Sounds of sight—

Sights of touch—

Touches of sound.
I become rebalanced—
My perceptions laced with gentleness—
Seeing past the pained behaviors to the beauty hiding—often frightened—hiding—
Yearning to be discovered.
Yearning to feel enoughness—
I reach through and offer a hand—
Cautious to just offer—and send acceptance—
So there will be enough feeling of safety to risk a response—
And perhaps I may share the place between breaths—
Between night and day—
So we can celebrate our connectedness."

David opened his eyes, took a deep breath, and looked at the monk.

"I've started to wonder if I'm going into trance and am hallucinating. It comes and goes, but seems to be happening more frequently. It's something like a result of my meditating."

The monk looked at David, covering up his surprise. "Tell me more," he said, leaning forward.

"Well, all of a sudden I see glimpses of people, people I've never seen before, looking at me as if through a window. The way they look makes me feel like what they see is not clear or in focus. After they look, they move, often followed by a different person. There seems to be both males and females. A few nights ago I had trouble sleeping. I got up and meditated. After a while, a male torso appeared, looked at me and said 'Hello!' I was startled. I said 'Hello' back, not out loud, but in my mind.' He smiled. He said, 'Welcome to my dimension. Not many of you enter here. You have learned to open a portal. You've been here before. Do you remember?' I shook my head. 'Ah, it is not unusual that you don't remember—too bad. Visiting here allows learning new perspectives of existence in your plain. I am inviting you to visit us, to become a Traveler.'

When the man paused, I knew my thoughts were jumbled. 'Could,' I said, 'we talk a little more about it?'

The man smiled. 'I'll be in touch.' There was a bright flash, then a pinprick of light that slowly faded. "What do you think?"

The monk was sitting on the edge of his seat. "You must accept the invitation! Many of us have searched, but few have found a way. And you were invited!" The monk shook his head in disbelief.

- - - - - - - - - -

The Man thought of the monk's reaction on his way home. When he arrived, he kicked off his shoes and sat in his most comfortable chair. He breathed in several deep abdominal breaths and started to feel relaxed.

"I wonder what he meant by a different plain," he mumbled to himself.

As he grew relaxed, he remembered some thoughts and questions he had on an airplane flight. He had looked down and seen tiny lines that were roads. He was aware that when he was far away, objects looked very small, if seen at all.

As the plane came closer to the earth, he focused on a building. It looked small. He knew if he had been standing in front of the building it would seem very large. Inside, furniture and objects of all sizes would be seen.

"Yes." He heard a voice. "You know when you are very large, small things may not be visible to you. You know that there is no such thing as solid and that a piece of furniture is made up of sub-atomic particles held together in empty space—the micro world in your universe. And you look at the night sky and see dots, a macro world where you could possibly be part of a piece of furniture in a different place. Macro world or micro world. They both exist at the same time. You are immense and you interact with other universes, sometimes giving birth to more universes. If you prick your finger, the drop of blood contains its own world. In addition, parallel universes exist at the same time. The images you saw were from the parallel universe existing in the same space you occupy except at different vibrations, unseen by your finiteness."

The voice became silent. He looked around to see if he could see anything. He shook his head and rubbed his eyes. Was he dreaming?

The next day he rode the subway and got off at his transfer stop. Knowing he had five minutes until his train arrived, he went to the coffee bar. "Black, no cream or sugar." The barista nodded and turned.

A man tapped him on the shoulder. He turned, and the man said, "You are The Traveler and have been invited. If you choose to come, follow me."

The man turned and walked toward a stairway. The Traveler followed him down a flight of stairs. The man walked up to a lone subway car and nodded his head at the open door. The Traveler walked in and sat down in the empty car. "Where are we going?" The man smiled as the door closed. "We will travel a great distance in what you call a short time."

There seemed to be a slight movement and the door opened. "We are here."

The train had stopped in front of an old movie theater. The man led him to a path in front of the building and pointed up to the crest of a hill. "Follow the path. You will come to a building. You are expected."

CHAPTER TWO

....

THE POWER

The Traveler had reached the building. It seemed strange to find such a modern looking building placed in what seemed to be at least an hour from any main road, surrounded by nothing but desert.

A man in a flowing red robe opened the large stainless steel doors and beckoned The Traveler to come in. He led The Traveler down a corridor lined with windows of colored glass. The reds, greens, and yellows bounced off the leader's robe and the white marble floor and walls. The Traveler began to experience a sense of movement in addition to the walking forward. The twinkling rays of colors seemed to be moving faster than he was, creating a sensation of floating.

They arrived at a large central hall. A translucent white dome made up the ceiling. Behind the dome could be seen the shadowy shape of a pyramid. The leader moved toward the center of the room. The floor tiles were in the form of a sunburst emitting from a circle in the center of the room. The tiles were polished marble alternating in black and white. When the leader and The Traveler reached the center of the room, the leader turned to The Traveler. They looked into each other's eyes for a moment—exploring the mystery revealed in that short period of time.

The Traveler spoke, "I was invited."

"I know," answered the leader. "Please sit here until you are called." The Traveler looked around. Behind him was a modern chrome chair with a leather seat and back. He had not seen the chair before, yet he felt no surprise. He sat, adjusting his body into the chair. The chair seemed to support him fully and comfortably. He breathed deeply in his nose and exhaled through his mouth. After a few breaths, he seemed at one with the chair. He re-experienced the sensation of movement—of floating as he did in the corridor. A sense of peace came over him. He felt safe and let go. The relaxation had a tingle of delight that reminded him of sexual pleasure. He closed his eyes.

The soft touch startled him. The bright white of the soft material almost emitted a light from her robe. Her tan skin was startling next to the white cloth. Her jet black hair reached to her waist. Her eyes were large and gentle. He felt dizzy for a moment, as if her presence was surrounding him, enveloping him, taking energy from him. The sensation only lasted a moment, yet he felt a link with her, connected in some way, a mixture of peace, sensuality, pleasure, calm, oneness, but most of all, trust. It was a given. He knew. He was now vulnerable to her. He was almost certain she would not violate his trust. They moved together toward another corridor. They did not walk, but moved together. It did not take long to get there, yet the height of ecstasy was greater and more intense than he had ever experienced in his life. At the edge of the corridor he heard her voice coming more from inside his head than through his ears. The voice said, "You must go this way alone." He knew the intensity of the energy could damage his essence if he stayed with her too long. The intense pleasure would quickly turn to pain. He knew. From her. He felt her leaving him. He was different. There was no void. He had expected a void. He knew he would desire a re-experience. Then he knew. It would always be with him to draw upon when he chose.

CHAPTER THREE

....

HALL OF DELIGHTS

He moved down the corridor. Again, he felt the movement sensation. There were no lighted windows. The corridor was lit, but there was no light source. There was something else. The Traveler stopped fighting and let go. He focused his energy onto the new presence. He was curious, not frightened. He wanted to know. What was it? He felt the tension knot in the back of his neck. He could hear her speak to him. Her voice was soothing. "Your energy is blocked. You will feel me touch it away. Do not turn around. Keep your movement forward and see me. Allow yourself to picture me touching your neck." At first nothing came to him. Then slowly, like an old TV set warming up, a picture started to form in his mind. It was fuzzy, and the details were not clear. She spoke again, "Very good. You are beginning. Allow yourself to see me." The details started to sharpen. He could see her coming toward him. He was viewing the scene from slightly behind and above himself. She moved closer to him. When directly behind him, she took a deep breath, looked upward, her hands and arms hanging limply next to her body. The robe, again, seemed to emit a light, setting off her darkened skin and intensely black hair. Her breasts pushed against the material. He felt his chest tighten. The beauty of the picture surprised him. He could hear her whisper, "Let go." He took deep breaths in his nose and out his mouth, and the tightness in his chest was gone. She whispered, "Your skin—your entire body—is filled with sensory receptors. Let them feel! Let them experience! Let them listen!" Again the voice was floating more in his head than coming in his ears. He became aware he was fighting. He started to become aware his muscles were much tenser than he thought. "Concentrate on seeing me," sounded a melody. He watched her slowly raise her hands. He started to feel his body sense her essence.

He could feel her essence meeting his as she moved slightly closer, laying her hands on his shoulders near his neck. The entire back of his body tingled.

He watched her hands move up and down his neck, over his shoulders and down his back. She seemed to be rubbing only in one direction. He could feel a warm tingling sensation where she was touching him. Suddenly he felt himself letting go. It was as if a dam had broken inside him, and the water had been a weight pressing against his body. He felt the sensation of his body deflating—collapsing. "That's good." Her voice was turning to music. There were no words and yet he understood the music. His senses were waking up as the stiffening presence left. First yawning—stretching—then alert—alive—listening—feeling! He could feel the air playing against his body. He was surprised how vivid he could feel it! Floating—riding—feeling!

He saw her body become transparent, and for the first time saw his essence. It was floating—a movement—and at the neck her hands were also transparent—her essence visible—also flowing—both flowing in the same direction. The movement of her essence increased the speed of his essence—the movement of his essence increased the speed of her essence. "You are becoming ready to hear," spoke the music. The pleasure from the music was intense. He closed his internal eyes and concentrated on listening. He remembered his question. What was the new presence? He wanted to know. He listened for his answer. He could feel it all around him. It was very different from the ecstatic, erotic feeling he sensed with her. It felt energizing, alerting all his sensory systems to an even higher pitch. He felt movement—swirling—whirling around him. He felt it brush against him. It was moving with tremendous speed, touching him again, then again. He felt his essence moving faster and faster. He thought he would fly apart. How could anything flow this fast? He thought he had reached his limit. He heard her music, "Why do you choose to limit yourself? Let go—let go—oooooo."

It moved in again and again—deeper each time. He sensed it was he that was putting on the brake. He was riding himself in first gear with the brake on. He now knew. WHY? What was he afraid of? I'm going fast enough," he shouted.

"Do not be afraid." The chamber echoed the music.

"I want to let go. I'm trying."

"Don't try—you are—you already are there—stop trying and be—by becoming what you already are."

The sounds reminded him of the music of Rimsky-Korsakov. Could it be that he too had heard her voice? Scheherazade! He concentrated on the last notes—racing—the power—the energy—the hurrying seemed to slow down. Everything seemed calmer, yet he could feel the energy, the power, growing stronger. He concentrated on that which he was feeling, realizing what was happening. When he stopped trying, he let go. The speed was fast, like a wheel moving rapidly. It seemed as if it was not moving at all. He allowed himself to go faster, no longer feeling as if he would fly apart. The speed was unifying. It made him whole. It was calming and powerful. He felt it move him faster and faster. Again he listened. Had he heard something? Faster and faster. It was a hum. Faster and faster. A moaning hum. Was it a group chanting a sacred ohm? No, but maybe this is what some had heard. Faster—faster. A power plant!! It was the hum of a power plant—the sound of moving energy. He was connected with infinite wisdom and infinite intelligence!

CHAPTER FOUR

··

THE FLAME

The elation was with him when he left the hall of delights. The inner chamber was darkened. As he looked around him, he was reminded of a giant wagon wheel with the inner central chamber at the hub and the corridors leading away like hollow spokes. For a moment he seemed to detect movement—movement of the entire outer corridor entrances moving slowly to the left where the hub could be moving to the right. He tried to be more alert, but noticed nothing. There were only two hallways lit, the one that led to his private space and another. He again felt the sensation of floating as his movement went down the corridor. The lights seemed to be moving slightly, and he started to feel disoriented. A strange feeling started to come over him, a combination of disappointment, guilt and despair. How could this be? He had been so high—so free, in touch with infinite wisdom and intelligence. It seemed impossible that the elation could be transitory and disappear so rapidly. He could feel his movements slow. Everything seemed an effort—moving, even breathing. He sighed. The sound he heard was full of pain. Had he uttered it? He started remembering incidents long forgotten—minor incidents when he had disappointed someone or made a mistake, and felt shame. A part of him transcended. It urged him to get out of the corridor. This was a destructive place. His rational self knew the irrelevance of the things that were flashing before him—the non-productivity of it. Yet another heavy repressive force slowed him even more, almost forcing him to listen to the negative sounds that started to accompany the picture. The feelings grew more intense. A great sadness came over him. His feelings of worthlessness were almost overwhelming. Then he saw it. It was a light off to the side, dancing like a flame. The air had a deadening, but pleasant, odor. Between him and the light was a gradual funnel-like surface, sliding to a place unseeable. He felt he should try to get to the flame, but he knew—one slip—and he would be in the funnel. All his senses were yelling, "NO! STOP!" Yet he felt a compulsion to move toward the flame. He remembered seeing a moth fly into a flame and destroy itself. He knew he must stop. Fastened on the wall was a type of handle. He grabbed onto it and crumpled to the floor.

"I won't listen," he screamed, holding on to the handle, crouching his body around him in a fetal position. He mustered his strength and tried to yell 'HELP' but no sound came out. Feelings of cruel laughter wafted over him as if amused at his pain and helplessness. The laughter, the source of the laughter, was urging him to the flame. He held on tighter and forced his eyes shut. The laughter rang out louder, echoing down the hall. He tried to move away from the pit, but it felt as if he were a piece of metal too close to a magnet. He knew if he got any closer he'd be pulled in. He tried to move away but the force holding him there was too strong. He was using all his strength to hold on, feeling himself getting weaker. He thought of her music fighting to let it in his head. He tried again to yell. A little feeble sound came out. "HELP!"

The laughter turned to a snarl. "HOW DARE YOU OPPOSE ME?"

He looked up. He felt frozen with terror. A shadow with red glowing eyes was beginning to descend upon him. "I didn't do anything wrong," he almost whispered to himself. A mixture of cruel laughter and snarls came from the thing. "LET GO," it screamed. "NO! NO! NO! NO!" he responded desperately.

He could sense his very essence being whipped, brutalized. Yet he felt no pain to his physical body. The whipping continued. He felt helpless. All he knew was he must hold on.

It seemed like hours later. It was the comfort of sleep through exhaustion that protected him. He moved slightly. He did not feel the pull upon him, the kind of pull that feels as if the gravity is increased, making simple movements difficult. He looked around himself cautiously. The thing was not there. He glanced at the flame.

He felt a tug of attraction. He quickly looked away. He backed away a few movements, stood up, and ran back down the corridor. He tired very quickly. Instead of getting closer to the entrance, it seemed as if he were growing smaller and the entrance moving farther away. He slowed to a brisk walk and tried to catch his breath. He started to remember the music of her voice and the pleasure he felt. He started to feel stronger.

He also felt he would not be able to get out by himself. He gathered his strength and yelled "HELP!" at the top of his lungs. He yelled again and again. Suddenly he felt exhausted again. He yelled one more time, then lay down and closed his eyes.

He woke, fully refreshed. He stirred, stretched and looked around. The strangeness seemed gone. He looked up and down the corridor, and started again to return, but hesitated. He looked at the other end—the direction of the unknown. He thought of her voice and his feelings grew stronger. He focused on the pleasant things, the excitement of discovery and the sheer joy of understanding. Was he an explorer? "Who am I?" he asked. "What am I?" he thought.

Without knowing it, he was focusing his internal energy on his questions. He could feel tugs of energy brushing against him. He listened intensely. The sound of a high-pitched bird coupled with the scent of burning wood entered his senses. A swirl of smoke danced before him. Then—the music—the high keys of the piano—"You're changing—it's OK—Let go—Let Go-ooooo."

He closed his eyes and felt a rush of wind. He felt his essence growing stronger—as if it had been deflated and was being refilled.

The wind rushed. He heard a faint sound of the hum around him again. It got louder as he stopped fighting. It was easier this time. Remembering the flame, he tensed up. Was this a trick? The smell of burning wood? The Flame?

He opened his eyes. It was as if he was in the center of a funnel of a tornado. Choosing to feel relaxed, he closed his eyes again and started to hear the hum. He started to imitate the sound. Ohmmmmmmmmmmmmmmm. Olmmmmmmmmmm. He sat and rocked back and forth until his eyes closed. Olmmmmmmmm went the energy as it whisked around and through him. OLMMMMMM.

He rocked. Olmmmmmmmm . . . he hummed and felt peaceful. He relaxed more and more. Connection—infinite wisdom—intelligence. OLMMMMM . . . OLMMMMM

He awoke suddenly as if something had startled him. He was still in the corridor. It was time to move. There was something different about the lighting. He seemed to be able to pick up sensory cues, not available to him before. Maybe he was just paying closer attention. He looked forward to the unknown end of the corridor—then definitely stepped in that direction. He walked briskly. He had decided his direction.

CHAPTER FIVE

THE ENTRANCE

What at first seemed a long way passed quickly. He was moving so rapidly he felt he should slow down. No, he decided, keep moving. It is a time for moving. The end of the corridor was in view. Giant red colored wooden doors, framed in gold—old fashioned yet new, were in front of him. The corridor had widened and had grown taller. He got to the base of the doors and looked up. The doors were at least twenty feet high and fifteen feet wide. He looked around himself. Directly in front of the door was the sunburst with the alternating black and white tiles moving out and under the door. He moved and stood directly on the sun symbol—looked around—and then yelled in a strong voice: 'I AM THE TRAVELER—I HAVE BEEN INVITED!"

He waited. Nothing happened. He thought if he concentrated harder and focused his energy the door would open. He wished for the door to open. His belief was unshakable. He knew if he believed strongly enough, it would open. He could feel all his energy concentrating. "OPEN!" he commanded.

Nothing happened. He was puzzled. Was he doing something wrong? He could feel her presence and was elated. The music tinkled. "You are doing nothing wrong . . . You are doing nothing wrong. What is wrong is that you are doing nothing." The melody floated in and out of his head, and then it was gone, as suddenly as it appeared.

He walked up to the door and pounded on it. The knock was so faint, if heard would not be taken seriously.

He moved back and studied the door. The handle was up about nine or ten feet. It jutted out and hooked to one side like the letter "L."

The carvings were ornate and beautiful. All the gold work was also done in a way that expressed the Love of Beauty. He started to experience a feeling of embarrassment for even attempting to try to open the door. 'WHO AM I TO ENTER HERE' he thought.

"NO, STOP," he felt her essence. 'PUT THOSE FEELINGS AWAY—OUT . . . OUT!!'

"Open yourself to me!"

He was surprised at her alarm. "Now, Now!" she urged.

He closed his eyes and focused on clearing his head of the feelings of unworthiness. He remembered her music—Olmmmmmm—the feeling of being filled. He filled the inner void with positive thoughts. He looked up. She stood in front of him. Her softness—her flowing movement—the black hair against the silk-like white garment. The material flowing with her body—accenting her excitement. His head was swimming. He could feel his breath tighten. He looked at her eyes and was taken back by the terror he saw there. "What's the matter?" he asked. She ran to him. Her body flowed into his. He held her close to him. She was trembling.

She whispered to him, "The Thing—The Flame—get their power from the energy of those kinds of thoughts. Without them, they cannot influence you. Please do not give them power."

"I only said . . ."

"STOP—Don't"—she was terrified.

"Your essence and mine have touched. What you do influences me. Your seemingly harmless negative thoughts contain powerful seeds of destruction. The positive energy needed to remove them is extremely out of proportion to what you would expect. Avoid them! It is not possible at all times, but you must be alert. Do not let them in."

He held her. Their essences blended—moving back and forth into each other's physical space. What he needed was her pleasure. What she needed was his pleasure. They nurtured each other. A pink mist of the pleasure wrapped around them, lifting them gently, providing comfort. They both felt protected because each chose to draw on a new source of strength already existing inside themselves.

The strength did not come from each other, but was already there— waiting to be discovered. They wrapped the pink mist around them and slept.

When he awoke, he was alone, curled upon the floor on the symbol of the sun. He remembered the melody. "You are doing nothing wrong— what is wrong—you are doing nothing." He stood, stretched and studied the door. He knew his belief was important—belief in himself to overcome this obstacle. He also knew belief without action would yield nothing. What could he do? He looked around the hall. There were a few pieces of furniture: a small, low table, a plant on a stand, a very large vase, and a low-legged cabinet with glass front doors. All looked very fragile and old.

How? Need I sneak in? Is there a back door?

"NO!" It was a shout. "Go by the front."

He examined the floor near the door. There were slight scratches on the floor from the door opening. It looked as if some of the scratches were very old. It was obvious the door opened, and had been opened many times before, but how? There must be a way, he thought.

He rumbled around in the glass front cabinet. Nothing here. He thought of moving it to the door and climbing up. He realized he could damage the piece, and somehow it didn't seem like the appropriate way. Other travelers must get to this point and get in. How? HOW? He looked in the giant vase. It was almost as tall as he was. He could not see the bottom in the darkness of its depths. He explored the chamber to no avail. He sat and looked around him again. He thought of ripping his clothing into shreds, making a loop and throwing it up and pulling on it. That might work!!

Something held him back. Well, if that's all I have, I could try it, he thought. He explored the room once again. When he got to the vase, he gently tipped it over onto its side and crawled in, feeling along the way. He pulled his hands back quickly. He had touched something-perhaps a snake. He reached in again and drew out a long nylon rope. He carefully tipped the vase back to its original position. He then looked at the rope. One end had a loop in it. After several tries, the rope swung over the handle of the door. He pulled. The handle moved with very little effort. He heard a click and the door opened slightly. He shook the rope off the handle, rolled it up, and placed it back in the jar. A shaft of light was slicing through the door opening, looking thick enough to touch. He walked toward the open door.

CHAPTER SIX

THE PLACE OF NEW AWARENESS

He pulled lightly on the edge of the door, testing its weight. To his surprise, the door moved easily, as if in perfect balance.

The Traveler hesitated for a moment, and then walked through. At first the light seemed so intense that everything around him seemed to be glowing a bright orange softened by a thick fog of soft yellows. Gradually his eyes adjusted.

The temperature seemed warmer. A soft breeze danced about him fluffing his garments and caressing his skin. The breeze gradually lessened and disappeared. He looked at the door behind him. It was as ornate on this side as it was on the other. He could only see blackness on the other side of the door through the opening.

He was in a courtyard with winding paths that passed by bushes and plants of intense colors and varieties. Almost none of the plants looked familiar to him. Around the edges was a wall of continuous stone buildings. There were several doors and many windows. The light overhead was an intense soft yellow emanating from a mist similar to a slowly moving cloud. The Traveler could not tell if the area was in or out of doors. He knew he had never before been in this kind of environment.

"Welcome!" The Voice, although soft and deeply melodious, startled him. He turned quickly. The man standing a little away from him seemed somehow—different. He couldn't quite put his finger on it. His hair was quite long, straight to his shoulders, then curling slightly. He had a trimmed mustache and a short beard that came to a point. His entire body seemed slightly oversized, without being out of proportion. He wore a robe of a material that appeared extremely soft. The man approached The Traveler. As he moved, the colors in the robe changed. It seemed to have no color of its own, but absorbed and reflected the colors of the surroundings in a manner that seemed deceptively natural.

"You have traveled far," rang his voice in a deep, rich tone. Their eyes met. For a moment, The Traveler felt faint. He experienced himself as becoming microscopic in size and moving at an extreme speed toward the eyes of the man, as if floating through space toward bright objects. The sensation only lasted a moment.

He re-focused on the eyes of the man in the robe. Something had happened. It was as if, in that brief second—they had somehow communicated with each other. He experienced understanding. This stranger had moved into the innermost parts of his psyche, understanding the hidden beauty alongside the pain, scars, and exhilarations that seemed to be all part of his living process. The Traveler felt a great sense of relief.

The man spoke: "Those who come this far are few. You can rest here awhile and return. You may also choose to stay awhile. The longer you stay, the more difficult it will be to return. You may also choose to continue your journey. If you stay here for a while, there is a risk. This is a place of reflection. In this space you will discover a new awareness—you will learn to view things from still another perspective. You will develop a new ability to understand."

"Why is that a risk?"

"Because," answered the man, "you will be changed. You cannot truly understand without being changed. I cannot tell you what that change will do to you or where it will lead. I can tell you what is now familiar to you, and comfortable, will no longer do what it has for you in the past. If you choose to understand, you will no longer fit in the space where you have been. I can also tell you that the change will bring about some discomfort for you. I do not know if you will arrive at a new comfort level in the new dimension. You must be aware of this risk when you make your decision."

The Traveler's first impulse was to blurt out that he wanted to move on—yet he felt no sense of urgency. A calmness came over him. He was experiencing understanding. This was, indeed, a place of reflection.

"It is time for your refreshment. Come."

The Traveler followed. For a moment he felt he had transcended himself and looked down. He could see himself being led along one of the winding paths. From this view, he could see the design. The paths were all part of a jagged sunburst leading toward the center of the courtyard where a bright yellow disc made up a large clearing.

He moved back to himself. As they reached the bright yellow clearing he was surprised at its size. It was larger than he had expected.

They continued walking toward the center. It seemed somewhat transparent in spots with the same type of misty light emerging from an unfamiliar substance, held in by a glassy cover.

They walked to what seemed to be the center.

The man reached toward his neck and pulled a sunburst medallion from under his robe. It was hung from his neck by a string-like material that was almost undetectable.

He put two hands on the medallion. The Traveler heard a click. A portion of the floor opened up. The Man beckoned toward the stairs. The Traveler slowly moved down to a small landing, four steps down.

"Wait there." It was said in a tone of a gentle request that had the effect of an urgent command. He pointed to a comfortable looking chair.

The Traveler sat quickly.

The man wisked by him. The Traveler thought the robe had brushed against him as the man passed, yet he felt nothing.

The Traveler sensed the platform lowering. He was enveloped in bright yellow haze.

It cleared as he went lower. He looked above him. It looked exactly like the dome of the courtyard. As he came lower, he could see around him. He was not quite ready for what he saw.

The platform was lowering him into another courtyard identical to the one he left—or it seemed that way.

He could see the paths and the edge of the yellow disc below him. The difference was there seemed to be many people—some scurrying quickly about, some not moving at all.

The platform came to a stop.

"Ah, it is nice to have you join us," The Traveler could hear the figure clearly, but his eyes wouldn't focus, and felt heavy.

"Close your eyes. It is time for your refreshment. The house you live in is extremely fatigued. You have come a long way. There have been many obstacles. It is not good to make such a major decision without the refreshment of reflection."

The Traveler tried to protest, but his eyes closed. He felt—good—energized. He wasn't used to resting. He was rested enough. He wanted to keep going. Isn't that what got him this far?

"YES, we understand your urge. We also know of your journey. You will now experience refreshment."

He felt his clothing being removed. He felt warmth—as if he were in the sun.

Time, as he understood it, had no meaning. Occasionally he felt pressures applied to different parts of his body. He didn't know if he was sleeping or awake. He sensed something—a slight awareness—that was as if time were passing, but nothing like he ever experienced before.

He remembered her voice, teaching him to let go.

He remembered the speed and the sound of moving energy . . .

The echo of "Let Gooooo . . . ." Sounded in his head. He remembered the pink mist of pleasure. He felt himself smile.

He had become aware of the tenseness in his muscles. He realized how tight he was.

He felt the warmth. More pressure—like fingers pushing different spots gently, but firmly.

He became aware how hard he was resisting. He concentrated on her. What was he fighting?

He realized the warmth felt pleasurable to him. The pressure seemed to rid him of discomfort.

Little by little, different parts of his body loosened. Let Go? Easier said than done, he thought. It was hard, this way—at first . . .

The warmth and pressure continued.

All of a sudden, it was as if a valve had let go. Whatever did it, he went limp. His muscles felt strange. He knew he had to choose to let it happen.

He remembered what the voice had said. "The house you live in is extremely fatigued."

He saw himself pushing against a hurricane. He also understood the direction he was now going was not the direction he usually chose. He was so used to fighting the hurricane to get where he wanted to go, he now just assumed the hurricane would be in a direction that would keep him from getting there.

Warmth . . . Pressure . . .

Warmth . . .

He looked around inside himself.

The hurricane changed to a strong wind.

He saw the direction he wanted to go. He started to float in that direction.

Warmth . . . Pressure . . .

    Warmth . . . Pressure . . .

        Warmth . . .

For the first time he could remember, he felt the wind at his back.

Warmth: Pressure

Pleasure . . . .

He felt the energy float in and out of him, easily, gently.

    Warmth . . .

        Touch . . .

            Pleasure . . . .

moved in and out of his body, he knew his body was being repaired . . .

    Warmth . . .

        Energy . . . .

        Healing . . . .

Maybe he wasn't as gentle with himself as he thought . . .

    Warmth . . .

        Tingle . . .

        Touch . . .

His image of himself had been that of a fairly relaxed person . . .

    Warmth . . .

        Gentle . . .

Why did this feel so strange? A different direction—with the wind-

    Touch . . .

        Warmth . . .

He let himself float with the wind. It caressed him and cuddled him. The touching changed. He felt nurtured—cared for—he wasn't fighting. He was flowing—moving—part of his own energy floated in and out. It relaxed him even more.

The healing continued. His body was changing.

He felt himself transcend and float, basking in moving energy and warmth.

This, indeed, was refreshment.

This kind of refreshment was also . . . a new experience.

The Traveler opened his eyes. He was next to the partially opened door by which he had entered. The man in the robe was standing next to him.

"You are right," started The Traveler, "I am changing by staying here."

"Have you made a decision?"

"Yes, I want to continue my journey. My curiosity, my wanting to know, transcends all other feelings."

"So be it!! Show me your decision."

The Traveler thought for a moment. Ah! Doing was expected!

He turned and walked toward the door. He looked up and was aware there was no handle on this side.

His glance at the man in the robe communicated his understanding.

The Traveler pushed the door. It moved easily and closed softly with a quiet click.

The Traveler looked at the closed door. He felt a slight pang of anxiety, yet felt no regret.

"It is time to move on."

"Who—what—are you?! asked The Traveler.

The man smiled and a far-off look came into his eyes. "I have been chosen to work with you as your gardener. I am responsible for creating an environment for you to grow and change."

CHAPTER SEVEN

THE MAPMAKER

T he sound of his voice was changing. It was vibrating as if in an
     echo chamber.
     The Traveler felt as if he was semi-conscious, being lifted by
a mini tornado. "It is time for you to meet the Mapmaker," boomed the
voice, echoing through his head and body.

Shapes passed before him. Suddenly he was rushing along a roadmap
of his own life. A man, somewhat older than he, was guiding him.
Experiences, events, and people flashed by quickly turning into physical
maps. Each map overlay the next, flowing quickly before him.

He felt a sense of direction. For the first time he could see the parts
going together. Each map elicited a feeling.

He heard the voice of the Gardener.

"The evaluation and integration of energies takes time and
receptiveness. What have you learned from your living?"

There was a loud buzzing in his head.

The passing of former experiences and maps continued to flash before
him.

He abruptly came to the present. He felt exhilarated, almost giddy, as
if he had been drinking.

He looked toward the future and the Mapmaker.

"Will you share your maps with me?" The Traveler could feel
his question, only slightly thought, being transported. He was
communicating and receiving at a level he never thought possible—he
knew this was a time for learning. He alerted himself for the Mapmaker's
response. There were others there to also listen to the Mapmaker.

THE MAPMAKER'S RESPONSE:

"I will share my maps with you so you may find your way . . .
Rest with me awhile . . . Use the light of my lamp . . .
No, I will not journey with you . . .
Why do you insist? My road is not your road . . .
Why do you try to coerce me into believing my destination is
your destination?
Are you so blind you cannot realize my gift helps you find
your way . . . And others their way . . . with all ways being
different . . . Although some roads may be traveled together
for a way.
Do not impose what is good for you onto me, believing it is
good for me also. Accept my aid . . . what I do . . . without
condition. Let us enjoy our essence together.
Recognize I am a stop at your crossroad . . .
Invite me to join you . . . I may be traveling in the same
direction and may choose to join you.
I may also be traveling in a different direction . . . And choose
not to join you.
Allow me my choice. Enjoy my essence today. Tomorrow, I
too, am different."

"What wakes up," he asked, "when you are in the present moment?"
He glanced over the group, his yellow robe glistening in the light of the
candles surrounding him.

His eyes started to close slightly then—after a pause—he spoke
again. "We are asleep so often—yet we are not aware of our numbness.
When asleep, the sands of time still flow, never to be retrieved. The only
permanence is impermanence, so why do you choose to sleep? Why do
you choose numbness?"

He paused again. A gong sounded, and he took a deep breath—
moving his robe, catching the light differently, little spots dancing over
his person.

"This moment is, and will never be again! Are you fully present? Are
you here right now, appreciating this precious moment, this *nowness*?

Aliveness is to be embraced, like the most passionate lover, with the
intimacy of the moment."

The image of the Mapmaker faded and flowed into the image of the Gardener. "What have you learned about where you are going from your living?" continued his question.

"What have you learned?"

"What are you learning?"

"Where are you choosing to go?"

The Traveler felt saturated with experiences.

The Gardener alerted The Traveler—warning him. "You must remember your experiences, so write them, describing your new awareness. By reading them, it will help you stay awake."

The Gardener wrapped The Traveler in a soft garment, from head to toe. He placed him on a cushioned table. The reactivated experiences realized themselves within him. He was changing. Does the butterfly remember he was a caterpillar?

The change continued. The ferment within him continued to make changes. This process went on for a long time.

The Traveler started to wake. He felt the confinement around him. He pushed and struggled free of the material wrapped around him.

As he sat up he immediately became aware that all his senses seemed hyper-alert. Faint odors were distinguishable to him. He heard sounds not accessible to him before. He could actually see different forms of energy floating around him, and could distinguish between them.

He sensed a presence. He looked toward a large wing-back chair with the back toward him. He walked to the chair. The Gardener was sleeping, breathing softly.

The Traveler watched the energy dance around the Gardener, with an especially thick layer and concentrating of colors around his head.

He called to the Gardener without uttering any sounds.

The Gardener stirred, and opened his eyes. He smiled, stood up, and stretched. As he woke, the colors around him became more intense and seemed to be moving at a greater speed.

"You have integrated well," he said with a smile, as he examined The Traveler. "Let us walk in the garden," the guide said. "It is important to empty yourself of your talents. As you empty yourself in this manner, your essence becomes more transparent. There can be times when you are completely focused and emptied. When this happens, you will be as a piece of crystal. You will vibrate and connect directly with the source of sources . . . and be refilled to abundance with new and expanded talents.

It is only by using your resources to the fullest that expansion takes place. Your growth and satisfaction comes by using and sharing, not by conserving and hoarding.

It takes courage to use your talents to the fullest. The path is laden with obstacles—mainly composed of fears. These fears come in all forms, including fear of making mistakes, fear of displeasing others, fear of letting your competence show, fear of the unfamiliar. The most difficult fear to overcome is the fear of pleasing yourself and appreciating your own uniqueness.

As the transformation of expansion comes, a type of rebirth occurs, offering new opportunities and challenges. Healing, new wisdom, and added perspectives often lead to the recognition of new paradigms. Once a new paradigm is understood, all the old systems are obsolete. This is both frustrating and exciting, since it means beginning with everything being new, challenging talents to grow and change. May your crystal transformations be many!"

They conversed without talking—with The Traveler bringing a closure to many experiences and events, seeing new patterns, new dimensions, and new choices, always available, but unknown and unseen until now.

"Do you dare to visit the depths of yourself?" The Traveler nodded. "Then when you return, write a description of your trip."

The guide pointed to a stairway. As the guide faded, he asked, "Is darkness the absence of light, or is light the absence of darkness?"

CHAPTER EIGHT

THE TRAVELER'S REPORT

I have decided to visit the depths of myself with the question, Is darkness the absence of light, or is light the absence of darkness?

The stairs go down in a circular style. It is as if I could see for miles. I speak with a tone of protest—"But we have only two hours. We will not make it in time and be able to return." I also have doubts of my physical ability to weather the endless stairs.

The answer came to me without anyone speaking.

"If you went from the earth a short distance, gravity would pull you back with no effort on your part; is that not right? When you go inside, a force such as gravity will push you back out, without effort on your part."

Reassured, I started to descend the stairs.

The weight of my body put the stairs in motion. They started moving at a blurring speed, twirling, moving, rolling, ever downward, even though I stepped slowly—one step at a time—holding the railing to maintain my balance. Occasionally I came to a window. It seemed there were other spiral-like staircases descending as was mine—hanging like twisting worms from above.

At one point, it seemed we approached an area more lighted—and as we traveled through like a train passing through a small town and station at night, I sensed the movement of living images, moving through a dimension that contained living creatures, yet unaware of me or the others' presence, then again moving on.

We moved through five of these lighter dimensions, and then the stairways seemed to move closer together, finally intertwining with each other, twisting together like a rope.

Then they connected and grew, as if moving from the tail of a cornucopia or a conch shell.

It ultimately ended and my stairway, along with many others, seemed to line the edge of a gigantic cave. It reminded me of an extremely large auditorium, but empty. I moved through the small, round entrance from my stairway and realized that all the entrances looked alike. If I was to wander around, I would need to mark or code mine if I wanted to return to myself.

In my pocket I discovered a piece of yellow cloth with red heart markings on it. I pushed the cloth between two pieces of wood that were jammed together at the top of the opening.

I stepped away a few steps and looked. The little flag stood out distinctly. I moved toward the center of the cavern, walking normally, and moving with tremendous speed. I saw a tiny light and moved toward it.

An intense light beam was coming from below, focused into a crystal about the size of a man's fist. It was cut, and the light was broken into a rainbow of colors that were being flung into all directions of the darkened cavern.

A man in a hooded robe that touched the floor seemed to be attending the crystal. The stand it was upon was rotating very slowly as the lights emitted from the crystal changed direction.

He looked up. He seemed very old to me. With a gray beard and mustache, the contrast of the dark leathery skin was dramatic. His eyes were almost closed. I now was an arms-length away. His chin moved up slightly, and his eyes opened. They seemed to twinkle so. Was it the light reflecting from them? The color from the crystal bounced all over both of us.

He smiled. It seemed as if his face should crack, but it didn't. Rather, it seemed relaxed. Bright, even, healthy teeth showed through the smile.

"Welcome—and sit." I became conscious of a chair next to me. I was a little surprised, first at its appearance, then at its composition. It reminded me of an inexpensive hotel chair, made of chrome and vinyl. "It will serve your need for comfort," he said, and smiled again.

I sat. I was upright and my attitude alert. The seat supported me perfectly. "You have come a long way to discover. Very few descend this far. I congratulate you on your perseverance and courage."

"Perseverance, perhaps. I don't know about courage. I am driven by a curiosity, a need to know—and yet—I don't know what I am searching for."

"Ah." He smiled again and looked out into the void behind me. "That is part of your humanness, especially your unawareness of how much courage it has taken to descend this far." He focused his eyes directly into mine. "How may I assist you?"

"I don't know. I just knew it was time to descend. "I sense I am changing, and if I change, I might no longer have access."

"You sensed accurately." His tone was serious. "You have spent a significant portion of your life preparing, and your time for metamorphosis is near. It is only in your current state that you have access this way. In your new state there will be need to prepare that new state. In your current state, you have prepared well and completely. I am glad you came. It seems many prepare, and then do not come. Those that come too soon, and have not prepared well, understand only from that perspective. Others prepare with only one mode, and never come and never reach metamorphosis. You are ripe to absorb—to see—to understand, adding a depth that will travel with you when you change."

He became quiet. We just looked at each other. I felt warmth come over me, and it seemed like a void within me was filling. I sensed his question. "What would you like to know?" My mind seemed to go utterly blank.

He spoke. "You are discounting your questions because they seem trivial to you. Let me assure you it is that which seems trivial is of real importance. If those issues that are small are neglected, our container becomes like a sieve, full of holes. Each hole is a result of the neglected part of yourself that has been labeled as <u>unimportant</u>. All things are important. All have their time and season."

"Yes. It's like I have a valuable resource, and I don't want to waste it with unimportant discomforts."

"Unimportant discomforts are the signals and clues to the truly significant. For instance, your discomfort with a mother spanking a child, when traced, can lead to the strange ability of the human organism to annihilate others, and ultimately himself.

"Look into the crystal. Let yourself fly. Let yourself see. Let yourself understand."

The Traveler looked into the crystal and felt he was floating. Then words and visions became part of him.

<u>Flying</u>
My shadow keeps getting longer
As the sun starts to set—
I have something important to do—
Unknown to me yet.

I am on the edge of a new
transformation-
Ready to fly and try new
wings—again.
The joy of coming out of the cocoon-
Knowing the time is short-
Knowing the importance of enjoying
And noticing my now's-
Moment by moment-
And flying is doing something.

A chance to use the gift
of a new metamorphosis—beyond
my time and before my time—
And a request—an opportunity
to fill a special niche,
That even unnoticed, affects
The balance of the universe—
Like an encouraging word to an artist,
moves the universe one notch—
one click
that changes the events of historical
future.

Not all living offers clicks—
and when the opportunity—and
responsibility comes, it is important
to do what destiny suggests
so balance can be reshuffled.
Some have more opportunities than others
and must choose to improve or decrease
the quality of the human condition.

Click—Shadows—Sun Settings—
New Life—Wings
A full set—beautiful—flapping—
Lifting me—
Allowing my perception to change—
Letting the beauty of authenticity
show by
being myself—
with courage and love—
and gentleness—
a sword of gentleness
tempered by love and swung with courage.

Then there was a flash of light. I was back to the top of the stairway. There was a writing desk and an easy chair next to it. I wrote the report, as requested.

CHAPTER NINE

THE GIFT OF REFLECTION

"**I** will rest in the chair," he said, after completing his task. He closed his eyes and went into a deep sleep.

Waking, The Traveler sat up and stretched. As he opened his eyes he saw the guide standing next to him. "I must have taken a nap."

"Yes, you've been unconscious for quite a while. I thought you were going to awaken fully a few times. You started to stir. Everything was ready for you here. You seemed awake for a short period of time, then went unconscious again."

"I feel a little disoriented. Everything seems familiar, yet I seem unclear in my thinking. I remember, yet I don't remember."

"You've been gone long. You will remember as you reawaken. I am glad you have chosen to continue your journey. You have used much of your life being unconscious, both on this plain and the finite plain."

The Traveler looked at the guide. He shook his head as if to clear it of the fuzziness he felt.

"Come," said the guide.

He led The Traveler through an entrance made up of two pyramids that glowed and emitted a soft pink light.

Beyond a row of orange trees was a little pavilion. The Traveler realized his senses were also re-awakening. He could hear a sound like waves caressing a beach.

Inside there was a group of people, each with a garment similar to his guides, but made of a different material. The Traveler looked at his own garment, and it was the same as theirs.

The Traveler's guide led him to the center of the circle.

They are guides, as well as travelers, as you are. Right now, you are invisible to them. You must reveal yourself to them, so they may give you the gift of reflection.

Take the risk. This is a growing place. Your time grows shorter.

There was urgency in the guide's voice that the traveler hadn't heard before. The Traveler turned to ask for clarification, but the guide was gone.

The Traveler now had his senses working for him. He sensed danger and raised his arm. He found a shield on it that emitted an energy field, protecting himself.

One of the group seemed to emit a brighter glow than the others. The Traveler moved consciously toward him and lowered his shield slightly, enough so the other presence could sense his outline. The glowing presence reached up and gently touched the arm holding the shield, as a gesture inviting The Traveler to lower his shield.

He could hear the guide's words echo—"take the risk."

He lowered the shield. As he did, The Traveler watched it change into a mirror. It was a mirror that not only reflected images, but also feelings. He realized the danger he sensed was a reaction to fear, and he was sending out the signals he was receiving through the mirror of the shield.

He lowered the shield more. He felt a sense of love, acceptance, and caring.

A ray of light came into the room that drew The Traveler toward it. It warmed him and energized him. He wondered how he had gotten so tired and so suspicious.

He heard the guide's voice as if in an echo chamber:—"Reveal yourself . . . ."

The Traveler walked to the center of the circle. He dropped his shield completely. When he did, he noticed the outline of the shield was covered with helplessness and accommodation. It was mixed with gentleness and caring. There was a little fear at the base. He was confused by the energy it emitted.

The other travelers focused on him. The Traveler then removed his robe. At first he felt vulnerable and a little awkward.

The members of the group all held up mirrors so he could see himself.

He was surprised at what he saw.

As he revealed himself, he saw different images of himself in different mirrors. He was startled at many of the images, and was surprised that he was surprised.

He saw a warrior in a full suit of chain armor with a handsome sword.

He sensed a great sadness when he touched the sword. He had denied his own powers and strengths.

In his quest for understanding and gentleness, he had forgotten or denied—he had a sword. He knew he could injure others with it, as he had seen some do. He had put the powerful sword in its sheath, and refused to use it on his journey. He drew from the power of the sword without taking it out of the sheath. He became aware that this method of encounter took excess energy, and the sword sheath was now locked with fear.

Four or five members of the group recognized the dilemma. Each reached out and touched the sword, freeing it to move if The Traveler chose to do so.

The Traveler put his hand on the handle and drew it easily out of the sheath. As he looked at himself in the mirrors, he saw a transformation take place. When the sword was out of the sheath, a light emitted from it and it was absorbed in him, allowing him to see strength and power blend with gentleness and understanding.

It was an attractive glow.

He saw areas he wished to improve, and yet accepted all areas he saw as they were. He denied nothing.

When he saw fear, he shared it, and the fear dissipated.

When he saw anger, he acknowledged it, and discovered tools to channel its power.

When he acknowledged sadness, the pain underneath dissolved and left room for joy and pleasure.

The Traveler put his robe on and joined the circle.

Some of the other travelers also revealed themselves. When they did, the healing energy of the group shifted, and there was movement in the sharer. S/He was changed. As the sharer changed, so did the other travelers. All were affected by each other, each taking what they chose to learn from the feast of opportunity based on their need and readiness to let in the offered lessons.

When all who chose to work were done, the group joined hands.

A beam of white light enveloped them. A calming, healing energy flowed through them, aligning imbalances within them. The light faded, yet the energy increased as it passed through them. Their breathing seemed to aid in the flow, as if it pumped the energy to great speeds.

As the energy increased in speed, The Traveler understood his oneness with the others, each being a part of the other. Within himself, he could feel the energy flow through every part of him.

He suddenly realized he could direct the energy to focus on any part of the body he chose. His left shoulder seemed a little tight, so he directed the energy there. The energy continued to flow through his entire body, with an increase in activity around his shoulder. As the bright white energy flowed in the area of discomfort, the pain seemed to dull slightly and gave off a hint of gray. After a moment or two it returned to its lustrous brightness. When it did, the shoulder felt loose and supple.

At an unspoken signal, everyone disconnected from each other. Some just smiled, others hugged each other.

The Traveler hugged. He felt like the returning hug moved the energy around in a highly pleasurable manner.

He felt energized, yet calm.

CHAPTER TEN

THE PHYSICAL BODY

As The Traveler passed the pyramid entrance on the way out, he was greeted by his guide. "Ah, you're glowing! You've expanded yourself considerably. Good. You are now ready to continue."

The guide walked with The Traveler a long way before talking. Then he stopped, faced The Traveler, and looked directly in his eyes. The intensity of the power of the guide resulted in The Traveler feeling slightly light-headed.

"I'm concerned. Not only have you been unconscious on this plain, you have also been only semi-awake in the other. If your physical house is in distress, it sometimes distracts from our work here. If your physical body returns to a state without the energy of aliveness, our connection is also broken. Although you exist beyond the constraints of your physical body, your body is your current home. If you do not take care of it, it will shorten the time you have to learn and do, since both dimensions are connected."

The guide led him to a small area with a glasslike pool in the center.

The guide said, "Watch—and remember her—you may want to meet her sometime. She was given only the blue lace and black beans. Watch!"

He pointed at the pool. They both looked into the pool to see and hear.

Blue lace and black beans. That was all she had left, if you didn't count the soft, wavey hair hanging to her shoulders. The beams of sunlight coming through the trees wrapped around her body like golden ivy.

She hesitated, and then moved down the path toward the sound of the sea, yawns, hisses, and sighs calling her—again. She clung to the delicate blue lace in her left hand, the black beans tightly in her right.

At the edge of the treed area she came to the white sand with tan foam pushed by the water onto the beach. The beach pushing back, the foam swallowed up by a watery blueness that was of a color that made it difficult to see where the water ended and the sky began.

She stopped at the edge of the woods, waiting. Waiting and listening. She tilted her head to the left, as if focusing her listening, and hearing something unhearable, then bent over and put the handful of black beans in a small concave depression in the ground.

She then carefully laid out the blue lace onto the ground, showing its delicate design—with intricate circular patterns. She then gently placed the beans in a pattern known only to her on the lace.

She took a deep, deep breath, her breasts lifting, her abdomen moving in, and softly exhaled.

She then positioned herself onto the lace, lying on her back, her arms comfortably next to her, out a way from her body. She could hear the unhearable sound more clearly now—and closed her eyes. She could feel herself changing—then feeling the wind lift her as if she were a wisp of nothing but energy.

She could feel her form change, and began to float, and fly, her blue wings hardly distinguishable from the sky. They looked at each other. "I don't understand," said The Traveler. The guide smiled—"Just remember."

CHAPTER ELEVEN

THE CROSSING

An alarm sounded. Everyone moved toward the chasm. The Traveler moved to the front so he could see the activity. A beam of light appeared in the distance and moved to the gathered throng and bathed everyone in its softness. A sense of peace and calmness came over The Traveler as he absorbed the warmth. The Traveler sensed a presence near him and turned to find the guide standing next to him. Their energies connected as the gentle light bathed them. The light began to focus and the beam started to narrow. Curiosity changed to fear as The Traveler became aware that the beam had narrowed and was focusing on him alone. He hadn't expected this! He looked at the guide. He realized the guide had not expected him to be chosen at this time either. The Traveler heard the guide instructing him. "We have no influence here. It is from a universe beyond us. You will see a light, a tiny dot of a light. Use it to stay on the path. If you must go through the fog of despair, follow it, even if you no longer can see it. Visualize the light and follow it."

The guide then tied a slender cord around The Traveler's waist. It was slightly thicker than sewing thread and had a slight glow emitting from it. It was tied in the front in a bow, with an edge sticking out, making it easy to untie. Why a bow? asked The Traveler with his eyes. The guide's answer, "So you can easily untie it if you choose," puzzled The Traveler. Why would I want to untie it if it was my only link to this side of the chasm? "Remember that absolute despair is never without absolute pleasure near. Balance is possible. Even on this trip, balance is accessible to you."

The Traveler felt himself being lifted up, moved to the center of the chasm, then being lowered in the mist.

As he was lowered, he felt overwhelming sadness and despair. He felt he had no purpose—no direction. The darkness became intense, seeming almost solid, sucking hope out of him. The pain of loneliness was intense.

He felt the thread. "Hold on!" He remembered: "Absolute despair is never without absolute pleasure near." He thought, "Hold on! Balance is possible!"

He continued to move down. The mist turned into a slimy mire. He tried to swim to the side of the sticky muck among vines that attempted to pull him under the water, their barbed tentacles ripping his flesh, causing great pain as the rancid water polluted the wounds. He struggled to get out, gasping with not enough clean air to breathe, and the stench made him wretch.

There are shadows along the edge of this desolate place. They refuse to offer a hand, and act with disgust at his existence. He crawls along, wondering if there existed a place of sunshine and warmth. As he dared to allow some hope, a branch fell from a rotted tree, knocking him in a slippery pit of despair, infusing his soul. Rocks seemed to cling to his legs, and to climb out seemed impossible. Where is the music? Where is the dance? He sees a mound with hair and thinks it is a symbol of compassion. With pain, he moves in that direction.

As he brushes the hair aside, he uncovers a mound of maggots, making sounds that absorb life and joy out of the air, leaving only darkness and loneliness. The feeling of abandonment reigns.

All of a sudden he was moving upward. He could see little wormy shapes swimming all around, lighting the darkness. His mood didn't lighten, however. He felt as if he were drugged, not sure of his direction. He tried to recapture the good feeling when he felt a direction with the Mapmaker's maps. Instead, he saw maps of barriers he had faced and the negative feelings that accompanied them. He heard himself mumbling to himself.

I can feel them lurking nearby—
Hiding in the shadows, these hyena demons—
Watching—waiting for me to fall behind
Into the shadows.
They don't attack in the daylight
Still
Daylight comes and goes

At unexpected times.

Daylight—I discover I am only a few steps
From the edge—the yawning chasm—
Just there—neutral—not caring
If I fall in or not fall in.

Even if I watch my step
The world tilts
And I fall in—out of balance—
And fall—toward the darkness.

I've fallen before.
Sometimes I have slept as I traveled through the fog.
The mist of unknowing seeps into me
And I sleep to protect myself—numb—
I don't feel the pain—
And when I wake
The damage and mess is all around me
As if visiting a place that was hit by a tornado,
Except I was asleep in it as it whirled around me.

I start to clean up, then feel overwhelmed by
The desolation and task of rebuilding—again—
and it pushes me to the edge—again
and I live in fear of my world tilting, catching me off guard—
nothing to hold on to.

My stomach tightens.
I tear in frustration with sadness filling me.
I don't want to fall—
I don't want to numb—
I don't want to sleep.

I'll fall behind—again
Never there—in the front—very long—
Just long enough to qualify, but not long enough
To finish my creations—not long enough

To enjoy order—
Always doing catch-up.

I don't want to just do catch-up!
I feel bruised—and damaged—and scarred
From doing catch-up.
So much energy—from doing catch-up—
So much energy—expended—
And just as I catch up
The race begins again—
The others well rested and anxious to compete—
And I am already exhausted
From just getting there—
Taking the way of barriers—
The path full of obstacles not encountered
By the others—
So when we line up, my disadvantage
Is very great.

To just stay in the race is an accomplishment.
Every time I appear—again and again—
My competitors, my peers—are surprised—
Sometimes astonished.
I am still there—still growing—still running—
Unwilling to quit, but the price of sleeping, of numbing,
Is high.

The distracters are powerful.
Tangled papers have a gravity all their own.
So does the lack of financial fuel which is
So often wasted on the medicine
To induce numbing—
To reduce the pain—
A vicious cycle.

Maybe there are other ways to heal.
I want to heal—and compete—rested—
At my best.

If I can give it my best try, I will
Be satisfied with myself, knowing that
Knowledge gets forgotten when using
My energy to swim in the fog lost and numb.
That is when the demons come feed on me
And damage again that that was repaired,
And attack other parts of me also—
Slowing recovery—and sometimes
Doing damage that is not reparable.

I learn to move on anyway, unwilling
To surrender and stay in the darkness.
I pull myself into the light—and rest a moment
As they let go and slink back into the shadows.
I rest a moment and want to sleep, but I know
I must keep moving to get to the
Land of Nurturing.

The map changes so quickly, and what was in one place
Is no longer there—moved—changed shape and appearance.
I am determined to find it and rest there awhile—
Then challenge the paper mountains
and foreboding trails that must be traveled to
Get to the starting line again.

"Yes!" he thought. The starting line—breathe in—breathe!
The wormy lights increased in number. He could feel his mood changing, his curiosity coming back. As he watched the wiggling lights enter his body, new energy filled the black voids, recharging him.

He felt himself being flung up into space, then, gently, as if deposited, standing beside a calm sea that went as far as he could see. His wounds were healed. The sky was a soft orange twilight. It was difficult to know where one ended and the other began. He looked down. He was standing on mirror-like panels, reflecting his image.

He turned around and surveyed the landscape. The mirrors ended at a wall of mirrors in the far-off distance. There seemed to be an opening in the wall.

"Well, I guess I'll go there." As the thought entered his mind, he was there. Even though he had many surprises, this was different. He looked in the mirror and saw several images of himself looking back at him.

He looked up and saw a pinprick in the sky. "Go there," he thought, and immediately was standing on a giant circular object. There were several dots orbiting around the ball. Intuitively he knew it would not be wise to visit the dots in the distance.

He thought "Home" and was on a rocky path that was on a hill, leading up. He focused on the top of the hill, expecting to be there instantly. Nothing happened. Instead, he started to see a glimpse of his former life. He thought of the subway car, and guessed his last focus was a one-way ride out of that universe. He looked around. He was in the woods.

CHAPTER TWELVE

THE WOODS

He had been in the woods
hundreds of times-
and found his way-
The path looked familiar
but, in fact, he was lost.
It was deceptive-
looking familiar-
yet different-
a different time-
a different place-
and the more he relaxed-
thinking that the next turn
would be the right path
the deeper the shadows
became—until the trees
looked unfamiliar-
and he acknowledged he
was lost.
He was aware that the weather
was to change for the worse
in a short period of time-
winter descending
bringing its deathly beauty-
when people of wisdom
went to the warmth of their
cottage-
and rationed the food of the harvest

and burnt the wood
collected in fairer weather.

The woods were no longer
friendly—nor were they unfriendly-
just different—and unfamiliar.
These trees didn't know him-
or talk to him—even though he thought
he performed the right ritual.

He honored and respected all the trees,
but he was lost—and
began to sense the danger.
Off the path a bit too soon and
now lost. He was puzzled
more than frightened. He was
annoyed. He was confused.
He had a period of denying he
Was lost.

Yet he *was* lost—and
needed a new plan.
These strange woods seemed
to put a spell over him.
His memory of how to solve
problems when in a strange place
faded-
All his experiences that
contained answers seemed erased—beyond recall.
In this mist of non-remembering,
he slowed down
and imagined himself in a
modest cabin stocked with
food and heat-giving wood-
a place of familiarity and comfort.

He became aware he was numbing himself
and walking in a little circle-

and didn't seem able
to break the spell.

A crow appeared. He was
glad to see the black beauty
and shared some of his bread by
putting it apart from him and
waited. The curious crow, when he was far enough away,
took the offering and flew off.
It, too, was familiar, yet different.

So now what?
He listened to the crows talk to each other
not far from him—sharing their secrets in
their own special language—and he
wondered if he might
learn something by
observing and listening.

They seemed to have a strategy.
Perhaps they divided an area up
and explored it, sharing with the others
if they found anything of interest, either to
note the location or call the others to explore together.

What was he doing?
He needed to spring into action, work his plan!
What plan? He had no plan.
Action? To do what? Get more lost?
Was there something better beyond the woods,
Or was there just more woods?
Should he keep going or should he try to learn
how to survive where he was?

If he didn't do something soon, he sensed
he would be in serious danger.

He decided to meditate-
and regain his balance.
then he heard her voice:
you're doing nothing wrong.
What is wrong is you are doing nothing.
He sprang to awakeness—and moved on.

CHAPTER THIRTEEN

THE PLACE OF PRESENT MOMENTS

The Traveler stood at the fork in the road. Which direction? To go back was not an option. Both paths were inviting. A large oak tree separated the road, its roots covered by soft green grass. The road to the left led through a meadow of yellow flowers, waving, and seeming to be giving off their own light. The path curled into a bed or hills and disappeared behind a crest of red jagged rock shaped like a sinking ocean liner being swallowed up into a sea of yellow.

A path on the right went slightly down, then up until it was surrounded by a thick growth of green trees that faded into the shadows. On the way to the grove of trees were bushes and brambles, some of which seemed to bear berries or some sort of fruit.

The Traveler looked at both paths, and then walked to the base of the oak tree. He'd depend on the old technology to guide him, and sat on a flat stone that peeked through the grass. Facing the path he just traveled, he sat, crossed his legs, and closed his eyes. He'd wait until the light appeared in his mind's eye and note its direction. He posed his directional question, and then took some deep abdominal breaths. He resumed his normal breathing, relaxing any part of his body where he felt tension. Soon the darkness in his head had threads of gray, and then spots of light would appear and disappear. A bright light appeared, mainly from his right side. It appeared so suddenly and with such intensity it slightly startled him. It was if someone next to him had turned on a bright light. He was tempted to open his eyes and look, but he kept his eyes closed. The light seemed to move down and through his body, healing discomforts and injuries. Then, as suddenly as it appeared, it was gone. He waited a few moments, and then opened his eyes. "Well, to the right it is." He got up, stretched, and looked to his right. The yellow flowers seemed happy to him, waving in the breeze, bowing their welcome.

It didn't take him long to reach the curve that went behind the red rock. The change in that path was dramatic. It was now mainly loose piles of rubble, rocks that rolled and made it difficult to walk. In addition, the path went up, and sliding rocks made the climb challenging. Near the crest of the hill he saw an opening off to the side. The light was growing dim, and he looked to see if it might be a possible shelter for the night. He explored the small cave carefully, alert for animals that might choose to use it for a burrow. He prepared his bed, then settled in and went to sleep.

He was sleeping deeply when it happened. He could feel something shaking him and he became instantly awake and alert. It was the ground shaking. He could see some stars through the entrance of the cave when he heard a large cracking noise, followed by a rumble. Something came down in front of the cave and blocked his view of the stars. Then he was pelted by stones and rocks until he was buried. One of the stones knocked him unconscious.

He awoke, weighed down by rocks and soil. At first he saw nothing, then, in front of him he noticed a tiny light the size of the head of a pin. He tried to move toward the light, but without much success. He had a little space around his head, and was able to move his left arm in front of him. His right arm was more difficult to move. He reached over and dug the soil around his arm, pulled it, and the arm became free. It was difficult to breathe. He started digging toward the tiny spot of light. He moved slowly, since rapid movements seemed to stir up dust and choke him. It took a long time, but with patience and perseverance, he was able to move closer to the light.

Suddenly, there was another upheaval. It was as if the earth was changing direction. The pinprick of light seemed to be shifting, disappearing and reappearing in a different location. He could feel some boulders roll past him, moving below him. Then he could feel sandy soil around him, heavy, but movable. The light seemed farther away, and the environment was shifting. It became completely dark and confusing.

He waited, then calmed himself as he made an assessment of the situation. He'd have to find a way to get his direction and pull himself toward where he remembered the light to be. What had he been learning? He thought of the Mapmaker when he saw flashes of his life come together. The section of barriers that had to be overcome to continue on his path had been illustrated. He now recognized the role of his own perseverance and courage that had pulled him past barriers on his path when his goals were clear. He remembered her voice. "You are doing nothing wrong. What is wrong is that you are doing nothing." He reviewed the many sources of teaching, support, and encouragement he had on his journey, and then had feelings of gratitude and appreciation flood through him. At that moment, a shifting source of light appeared. A tiny shadow came through the pinprick, emitting a soft blue hue. He could see the blue butterfly wings and recognized the woman in the lace with the black beans.

He heard her instructions, requesting the thread around his waist. He reached through the sand until he found an end, and pulled. The thin cord came out. She took it and positioned it in a line toward the light. She then dropped beans along the cord. "These are your beans. Their light will guide you as you dig. They are made up of your own acts of compassion." Then her presence faded.

The Traveler started digging, pulling, scratching, and moving the dirt, little by little. He heard friendly laughter, as if laughing at the dirt trying to stop him. He smiled as he recalled objects he had challenged with success, and with another surge of energy, dug some more. It was time to dig!

He hit some difficult sections. He gritted his teeth and dug some more.

The light seemed to be getting closer. He thought, "Uncover the potential!" and dug some more.

Everything went dim, even his black beans. "Must be a time to rest," he murmured to himself. He caught his breath and rested until the glow from the beans returned. He heard himself whisper, "You can do it." He started digging again. Dig, dig, dig!

Only a pinprick of light. Closer! Closer! The edge. Open up. Breathe! Breathe! Pull out of the hole! Breathe!

The sun felt healing. It felt like the memory of long red hair brushing his body. The breeze was soothing, like a soft caress of a gentle hand. He lay still, then pulled his alertness together. He looked around to find himself in a meadow of clover, with a view of a valley before him. A path twisted down the hill, lined with fruit trees on both sides, ripe fruits hanging, inviting him to refresh himself.

But first The Traveler rested, drinking the breeze and absorbing the sun's nourishment. He closed his eyes and purposely relaxed his body one part at a time.

He sensed a presence. He opened his eyes to see a figure bending over him, a woman. Her long dark hair was framed by a shiny white garment, toga style, large gentle eyes and a soft smile that seemed full of compassion and comfort. It took him a few seconds before he was alert, just as she touched his chest, and spoke. "Not many reach this far. Welcome to the land of now. This is the place of present moments."

The Traveler sat up. She pointed to the rubble of rocks. "The red ones are heart disease. The gray ones are cancer. And the others . . ." she stopped and shrugged. "It doesn't matter. You're here. It is time to rest and refresh yourself. Come with me."

They walked down a path together to the edge of the grove of fruit trees. "I hope you take charge of refreshing yourself. This *is* the place of present moments."

For some reason unknown to him, he was not surprised to see different kinds of fruit growing from the same tree. He reached out and chose a large peach. As he touched it, he realized it was dead ripe, as if waiting for him to accept its offering.

He bit into the fruit. His dry mouth was filled with the sweet moisture, and unique in its pleasant flavor, satisfying in a way new to him. He instinctively knew there was no hurry, and let the flavor savor in his mouth. His hunger disappeared and his thirst was quenched as he slowly chewed and tasted, as if tasting and chewing for the first time. The old was now new. He could feel his strength returning—as if the sun was recharging his battery.

He started to feel a sense of excitement growing within him, his explorer self growing curious. She looked at him and smiled. "We can extend your summer, yet I can tell you feel the Autumn in the air—another challenge—what to explore-which direction to go," she laughed. She handed him a traveling bag. "It contains gifts for you." Her laughter turned to the sound of wind chimes—as she transformed into a butterfly and flew down the path.

The Traveler knew he had a little time before his sun would set.

The Traveler came out of the woods onto an open hilly plain—green as far as the eye could see, with patches of reds, oranges, yellows, blues and whites speckled among the landscape. Crevices of hills tucked into each other, suggesting shadows where the hills folded into each other.

About a hundred yards to the left was a crude wooden hut with a hay-thatched roof.

The Traveler headed for the hut, but saw no signs of life.

The doorway was framed in stones, and a door hung tilted to the left on leather hinges.

The Traveler knocked, waited, then pushed the door open. There was a rough-cut wooden table in the center of the single room, a mat of gray cloth stuffed with leaves and straw on the left side of the room next to the wall. Very much out of place, a modern looking leather recliner was sitting next to a small stone fireplace.

The Traveler sat in the chair, pushed it back as a footrest came up, and took a deep breath. The trip through the woods had been tiring. He put his head back and fell promptly asleep.

As he came out of the twilight of his sleep, he saw a shrunken gray-haired woman, completely in black, approach him. She reached out and touched his hand gently with bony, gnarled fingers, her hand covered with brown spots and a wart.

As the hand touched him, he felt a surge of energy flow through him. He could feel the fatigue in his muscles seep away, and a sense of lightness come over him. His mood brightened to the point he almost felt giddy.

He looked again at the woman as she withdrew her hand. Her appearance now matched his mood. She was young, with rosy cheeks and hair to match. A cream-colored soft linen garment fell softly over a firm, curved and youthful body.

The Traveler felt surprised that he felt no surprise.

Their conversation was without spoken words, and it was difficult to know who said what.

CHAPTER FOURTEEN

....

CONVERSATION

I am in the sunset of my life—where now?
How do I use the short time I have left?
A legacy—for who?
Joy and pleasure? My, how that has changed.
Sensual and sexual were one thing—now they are not connected
and different.
Sexual is such a small part of sensual but my, a disproportionate amount
of manic energy—like some foods that are
nutritionally dense and others that have lots of
calories and are nearly nutritionally bankrupt.

That much manic energy banishes night and death visits—
A positive energy that lights up the darkest place—day or night—
hot or cold—rich or poor—the brightness is a heaven among us—
allowing us to see our own beauty and gifts, not our shortcomings and
imperfections.
We all are imperfect, and we all have beauty—do you
Know what your beauty is? Your natural talent,
The ones you discount—and say—"anyone can do that:"
It's not true.
You are not telling a purposeful lie, you are just having a
difficult time seeing the truth.

You are having a difficult time seeing the truth—
The truth of your own beauty. You are not alone.
The funny part is that it is death that gives us light to see our own beauty.
An unlikely source, you say. I say, "unlikely source" also.

Then I realize it is against the backdrop of death that
the energy of life and its brightness become so easy to see—
to recognize the preciousness of the moment.
The Joy of Now!

It is Death that gives us light to see our own beauty.
It is the contrast of the figure—ground that gives us
the ability to see which was before unseen—
yet there it is in front of us.
Ah, so death is a friend of our perception—helping us see our world as finite
and forever—now—is never again, tomorrow is never there unless we go
through now first.
But isn't death—dark? Death is the absence of life.
Dark is the absence of light.
It is our perception that experiences that world—
as a place of light or a place of darkness.
I will die soon—or not so soon. What is important are the moments—
Strung together.

Then there was quiet—broken by music.

"Take the path to the left," said the music, "and take this stone. Beware of becoming intoxicated by the yellow flowers." She placed the tiny stone on the table, and seemed to fade away. The Traveler fell into a deep sleep.

He was awakened by a golden ray of morning sun slicing through a space between the boards of the hut.

He was lying on the straw and leaf filled bag. There was no modern chair, just a rough wood bench.

He stood up and stretched. On the center of the table was the stone the woman left him.

He looked out the door—seeing two paths, one going to the left and one heading straight toward the open fields.

The Traveler headed off to the path on his left, the stone in the left front pocket of his jacket.

CHAPTER FIFTEEN

THE PATH

The Traveler took the path to the left.

As he turned around a bend, he saw bright beams of light slicing through white fluffy clouds that seemed to be shining on a small nest of hills slightly to his left, illuminating the area as if it were emitting its own light. Just ahead was a fork in the path, both seeming to aim for the lit section of hills. The path on the right was lined by tiny yellow flowers. The path to the left seemed to head through a meadow, the grass so long it would be easy to lose the path. The Traveler was unhesitant as he took the left fork, avoiding the inviting flower-lined path.

Walking was difficult, and The Traveler would have to stop often and ponder his direction as he moved through the high grass.

The path became easier as the grass thinned out and got shorter. Then, after climbing a long, gradual hill, he came to a crest where the view was spectacular. He could see the sun glisten as it bounced off something shiny in what appeared to be a walled area on a hill far ahead. The Traveler took a deep breath, sat, and as he breathed in, he felt as if he were breathing in sunshine. As he did he felt as if he were hearing the sounds and the sights around him for the first time.

He saw details of tiny flowers, noticed the vegetation waving and smiling at him, heard the chorus of sounds around him in a new way, synchronized with the rhythm of his breathing and the movement of the earth. The changing scents were delicious—each making their offering for his pleasure.

He closed his eyes in a gesture of appreciation for the rich delights surrounding him, thankful that he could experience these pleasures, so often availed, yet unseen and unheard.

With a sense of fullness, he followed an ever-widening path, breathing in the wonder as it rolled before him.

There were trees everywhere, bending from the weight of their own fruit, and bushes filled with a variety of berries.

He filled his pack with a variety of fruit, then removed some to make the pack lighter. There was abundance all around him, and available to him for his bidding. He breathed in the ever-changing perfume as he slowly ate a piece of selected fruit, its taste pleasing his senses, its moisture eliminating his thirst, its aroma creating a moment of magical pleasure.

Occasionally he passed people who smiled and waved or greeted him in some gesture of friendliness. The energy around him was supportive and exhilarating.

Tasks that seemed difficult and chore-like became easy and pleasurable . . .

The Traveler came over the rise of the hill as the village appeared below. It was growing dark, with the evening lit only by stars in an almost moonless night.

The village appeared dark, with only one house lit. The house was made of twigs and logs, and the pale yellow light from candles slipped through openings in the walls and windows—slicing the blackness like a sword, slicing through with no one damaging or being damaged.

He could sense, rather than see, the path that led down—the path that would take him to this beacon in the night, take him to a warmth that would heal pain, salve wounds, and emit love.

There is magic in touch—the touch of one human making physical contact with another.

The Traveler moved carefully down the long hill, then followed the path to the tiny shelter that emitted the light.

He walked up to the door, following the twinkling light that came through the partially open space between the rough frame and the knurled wood of the door.

He did not knock. He pushed gently on the door that swung open easily, squeaking in delight the announcement of his arrival.

He hesitated a moment, then stepped into the candlelit room. There seemed to be candles everywhere, and the soft light was bright enough to make it difficult for him to see for a few moments.

The shadowy figure in the center of the room started to slowly uncover details as he became adjusted to the light.

At first her hair was long, straight, and red, then shoulder length and black, with curls, then short and white, then back to long, straight and red.

Her face changed as her hair changed, not abruptly, but softly moving from one shape to another—all with a warm smile and twinkling eyes—eyes that were full of stars—the smile as soft as rose petals.

The Traveler took in a deep breath. He took his knapsack off his shoulders and put it before her, kneeling, and uncoupled the two fasteners on either side of the light green canvas pack.

He opened it, reached in and pulled out a piece of very fine and almost transparent cloth, mostly pink, turning red nearer the edges—and trimmed with a shining blue and maroon velvet cord.

He stood up, then walked over to the woman, their eyes connecting. He watched as her eyes changed—shades of blues and browns, and even a darkness that was almost black, never losing the stars—always emitting softness and gentleness. He placed the material over them both, then took her into his arms. He stroked her hair with one hand and her back with his other. She wrapped her arm around his neck and nuzzled her head into his shoulder, her hand rubbing his arm.

The material turned into a pink mist, enveloping them, wrapping around them, creating a softness in their bodies that allowed their essences to intermingle, and as they became as one, a glow emerged from them—filling the room with understanding, gentleness and compassion.

When the first rays of morning sun warmed his face, he opened his eyes. He was lying on his stomach on a low bed, long red hair cascading past his cheek. She was lying on his back, and he became aware of her breath—a music that matched the hum of the universe—a finite sacred olm—and he listened as joy and peace flowed through him as he fell back to sleep.

CHAPTER SIXTEEN

THE PROPHECY

He was in the form of an eagle gliding. He looked down, in wisdom, seeing glimpses of potential—people united, wholeness and peace. Waves of positive energy, then released—another wave refreshed him.

As he moved ahead he saw a tiny dot coming toward him—and as the image got closer, he recognized her.

They floated—circling the air currents together—and he listened as she shared her visions and wishes—and he felt connected and a feeling of peace came over him as they flew toward the mountain bathed in orange light.

She said, "We have a choice."

The sacred vibration gave them a blessing—and they flew together.

"My wings are wide—I float with ease—with you," he said.

She smiled—and led him to see the shoreline with the path of the sun reaching over the water—inviting them.

"We have a choice—the land of the living or the land of the dead—"

"It didn't matter then," he said, "but now—let us celebrate living—"

Below were tents, with music floating and beckoning them—desiring their presence.

They descended into the tent and changed form.

He covered her in his pink sheet of gentleness—and the music pulsated through them—

inviting—pulling out each other's beauty—

blending and bending their energies—

and their softness combined—

created a new strength—

and both felt the beauty in them grow.

The lotus bloomed before them-

Born of their seed.
They stood and moved, as the rhythm of life increased—
And they knew it moved only in one direction—
So they chose to experience their nowness
together—
and follow the smoke from the fire—
twisting and turning within it.
The dance of wisps of smoke—pulsating with the rhythm of the drum—
Life moved on—
And they chose to experience its rhythm and flow—
Seeing, hearing, feeling—
Allowing numbness to fall by the road—
The flow together—
in the dance
in the rhythm
teaching them to feel the beauty around them—
inside them as well as outside—
And they held hands as they watched the sun set.

The Traveler woke up, feeling a little dazed, not quite ready to end his twilight trip. The images of his dreamy vision were already starting to fade, yet he struggled to keep the pleasurable sensations with him. He closed his eyes, attempting to see her again. He took a deep breath, fighting awakeness, and felt himself sinking again into the softness of this other dimension. He tried to picture her in the swirling darkness when he saw a pinpoint of light. He could feel himself move rapidly toward the light—faster and faster—then slowing as he could make out her figure in front of him, her garments flowing as she moved ahead, a soft blue light emerging from her. She sensed his presence and turned as he approached. He was enveloped in a pink mist and he was being held by her, tiny as a new baby looking into her face, feeling the warmth of her presence against him. She looked at him, smiling. He could feel himself being rocked, ever so gently.

"You are so new, so beautiful, so much potential waiting to happen. I must leave you for you to grow. I give you gifts, in love, that you may draw upon as you journey, but it must be your journey. Infinite wisdom and intelligence will be always with you if you choose to listen, and the right path will not always be the easy path. You will know the difference.

You will have the power to choose. You will always have the power to choose. Remember that, because there will be times it will feel you have no choice. My wish for you is to choose aliveness more often than numbness. Our time together has awakened you to the power of now. All gifts, even awakeness, have a cost. I value awakeness, so it is a bias." She smiled that soft, melting smile, her face glowing. "Enjoy your gifts." Her face appeared as if at an end of a tube, her image accelerating away, getting smaller and smaller, the light and her smiling face penetrating his consciousness.

He opened his eyes. He knew her visit was over. He felt curious again, and could feel his strength returning. He resisted the impulse to bring his knees to his chest and tighten his eyes. He knew it was time to stretch, and move, and ready himself to continue his journey. He felt catlike as he twisted his body, taking time to enjoy the stretch as he moved himself. He was twisting his neck when he saw it. The sparkling red and blue stones decorating the bag seemed to be signaling him. A soft pouch with drawstrings, the stones placed in a design that resembled a heartbeat. He knew it was full of gifts of love. He reached for the bag. It was just out of his grasp, and he seemed unable to move any closer, as if his body stopped working.

He felt a presence. He felt a smile—and slowly—he felt he was able to once more move his limbs. He reached for the bag and pulled it toward him, and placed it just under his left rib, where it would be safe. He knew he was traveling again. He relaxed and let himself enjoy the movement, wondering where he would emerge.

He'd been down this lane.
Yet, no path is ever the same
He was on a different life path.
He thought of his learnings.

The sign said One Way—
But it's often not noticed—
As we go on this life's journey—

Down the road—
We are moving,
Whether we are aware of it or not—
Moment by moment—

In one direction—
The missed sunset is gone forever—
The flower, unnoticed, disappears—
The opportunity
The Kiss
The Touch

Each moment is separate and precious—
Offered to be experienced—
A once in a lifetime offer.
It never comes again,
Never just like this.

Every moment is a new beginning—
A new choice.
And old habits of responses are choices—
The choice is ours—moment by moment—
How we respond-
How we take care of ourselves.
How we live,
How we experience this moment.

The Traveler continued moving, making observations, and paying attention on purpose. Around a bend, the path traveled in two different directions.

He followed the dusty path toward the pyramid in the distance. There was a rise in the path. At the crest of the hill, he saw a building in the gully. The old movie theater had a blinking marquee that announced "Travelers Admitted Free."

As he entered the theater he was surprised to see the man who met him at the subway. The man greeted The Traveler warmly.

"You are about to get a great gift. You'll like today's program. Please have a seat."

The Traveler looked around. It was as if he was in a field of expansive open ground with the sky overhead. Nearby was a simple writing desk. The man seemed excited. "Not . . . there. Here. The writing desk is for you when you return." He pointed to a stool. "You are to go on a trip before returning to your other place."

The Traveler sat on the stool, not sure what he was to do. The man continued, "I'm looking forward to hearing about this trip when you return. You'll leave when I close this door. Enjoy!" The man stepped through the doorway and closed the door.

THE TRIP
MY CHARIOT—
PULLED BY HARNESSED
CREATIVITY-
AND THE POWER OF
FEAR-
CONFINED—FOR A
CHANNELED FORCE
WHERE
IN UNISON-
ARE A TEAM
OF TWO GREAT HORSES-
ONE BLACK
ONE WHITE-
A MATCHED PAIR OF BEAUTY-
INTERTWINED-
AND WHEN PRANCING
TOGETHER
PULLS MY CHARIOT
OUT OF THIS PLAIN-
INTO EXHILARATING
SPACE—VISITING DEMONS
WHERE THEY LIVE-
FRIENDLY-
AND PASSING THROUGH
CLOUDS FULL OF MOONDUST-
ABSORBED INTO MY
BODY—HEALING-
AND TRANSFORMING
AS THE TWINKLING DUST IS ABSORBED
VISITING ON—AND OUT-
WITH CHANGED
PERSPECTIVES-

WHAT A WONDERFUL
WAY TO TRAVEL-
THE COSMIC WIND
RUSHING THROUGH MY HAIR-
ALTERNATE FLASHES
OF LIGHT AND DARK-
TIME SUSPENDED
AS I TRAVEL THROUGH
NIGHTS AND DAYS
TO A PLACE
OF REST AND COMFORT-
AN OASIS
IN THE UNIVERSE-
WHERE MY FORCES ARE BLENDED AND BENDED-
ENFOLDING ME WITH
GENTLENESS-
OPENING MY UNSEEING
EYES—CONNECTING
MY TOTAL
SELF AND BODY-
IN A COSMIC MIXMASTER
BLENDING THE EXPERIENCES
OF MY LIFE-
WITH STRONG EMOTIONS
USED AS SEASONING-
READY TO BAKE
IN A BEE HIVE
OVEN LACED WITH STARS
TIME PELLETS GENERATING
BY THIS COSMATION
MICROWAVE-ANCIENT
AND NEW-
I AM PREPARED IN
STAGES
PIECE AT A TIME
LAYER BY LAYER
THEN-
BACK TO MY CHARIOT

A BIT TRANSFORMED
SEEING MORE OF THE UNSEEN-
STARTING TO RECOGNIZE
THE MARKERS OF THE MUSES-
WHO WILL APPEAR-
IF I ASK FOR GUIDANCE-
IF I CAN SEE AND HEAR-
THEY ARE HERE
TO SEE AND HEAR-
AND A FORCE WRAPS AROUND
THE HORSES AND BLENDS THEM INTO
A DRAGON OF DELIGHT-
BEAUTIFUL IN ITS UGLINESS.
AND I REALIZE THE POWER COMES IN ANY
FORM I CHOOSE-
AND IT'S ALL FRIENDLY
IF I ALLOW IT TO BE
TAKING ME—WHERE?
ON A TRIP ABOVE
MYSELF-
IN AND OUT AT THE SAME TIME-
THE DEPTHS OF IN-
THE DISTANT PLANETS OUT-
IN AND OUT AT THE SAME TIME-
I HOLD THE REINS-
AS I STAND IN MY CHARIOT-
ORNATE AND PLAIN
GOING EVERYWHERE AND
NOWHERE-
SEEING EVERYTHING AND NOTHING.

AND THE COSMIC DUST ENTERS MY PHYSICAL BODY
HEALING—ALLOWING A LITTLE
MORE TIME
FOR MY ESSENCE TO
VISIT-
AND FLY WITH THE CROWS.

When he was done transcribing his experiences, the Traveler opened the door and left the theater. He was greeted by the man. "May I hear about the trip?"

The Traveler handed him a tablet. "This is my description of the trip. Hold on to it until I come back." The Traveler grinned.

The man seemed elated, then gestured toward a waiting subway car.

The Traveler entered and sat. He looked at the man and asked, "I'm going home? Won't people have missed me? I was gone a long time." He felt a little bump and the subway door opened.

The man laughed. "You will be home when you left. You've been in "*No time*" as you know it. You have been in "*Now time*." The voice laughed again.

The Traveler left the car and walked up the stairs, entered the area of his transfer stop, and walked to the coffee bar.

The barista turned with a coffee in his hand. "Here you are, sir. Black, no cream or sugar, just as you ordered."

The Traveler put money on the counter as he said, "Keep the change." He turned around and looked for the stairway. It was not there.

He reached up and touched his body just under his left rib and smiled. He knew he was full with gifts of love. He put his left hand in his pocket and found a small stone. He smiled. He wondered what he'd be invited to explore next. He'd be ready.

BOOK TWO

CHAPTER ONE

SPRING'S GIFT

S he put her book down, stretched, and walked through the door. From the porch she could hear the music, mainly drums, coming from the tiny town not far below.

This is the first time she heard the music in the daytime, and, being a stranger, was reluctant to explore the town at night. She turned, went back into the house and called, "Dad, where are you?"

"I'm in the den," came the response. Sue hurried to the den. Her father was sitting on a plush leather chair with his feet propped up on a matching hassock.

"The music is playing again. Are you feeling well enough to go explore? You could ride in the golf cart they left for you to use."

"No, I don't think so. I'm still recovering from my walk from the kitchen." She heard him chuckle. "Why don't you go without me? It is a safe area, and it's daylight. It's time you explored our new home area anyway. We will be here at least a year."

She shrugged. "All right. I'll give it a try." She glanced at herself in the mirror, liking the way she looked. Her trim body was accented by a soft blue sweater and tight jeans. Shining diamond earrings peeked through the dark shoulder length hair, glimmering like stars on a dark night.

She walked down the small hill to the tiny town area. The town square was full of people, many dancing as a small group of musicians played. The music was intoxicating.

"You don't need a partner to dance." The deep friendly voice came from behind her. She turned to be greeted by a warm smile. The man was about her age and was easy to look at.

"What's the occasion?" she asked, noticing his muscled body.

"We dance to welcome Spring. It is an important season for us. I know you arrived last week. How do you like our village?"

"I don't know. It's my first venture out. I was waiting for my father to feel better so we could go together, but that could be a long wait."

"Let me show you around. My name is Jeff. I went to school in the United States. What brings you here?" he asked as they started walking.

"My father. He has very bad heart disease. He did a lot of research and found out there are sections of the world that have virtually no heart disease. This is one of those areas. He thinks being here might help. I am reading a book now that he suggested. Is everyone vegetarian here?"

"Pretty much. No one eats meat. No dairy either. I had a hard time at first when I was in the United States. Everything to eat seemed to be meat or dairy based. Lots of salt and sugar, too, all not part of how I eat."

They were both quiet for a few moments. "How sick is your dad?"

"Very sick. He's talking about staying a year or more. I . . ." She hesitated. "I don't think he'll make it that long. He almost didn't survive the trip. He can hardly walk room to room without pain."

Jeff paused before he spoke. "My mother is—well—the town healer. I don't think you have a function like that back home." He smiled. "Sort of what you would call a medicine woman, or man. You would probably think that what she does is strange, but she has lots of good results with local people. I'd suggest that she visit your father, but he'd probably think of her as a Witch Doctor, and not be very receptive."

"Oh, I don't know. My father was a professor who taught about cultures all over the world. He laughs when some things he says seem very strange to me."

Jeff shrugged. "Well, it can't hurt. She might not be interested, though. His being from the United States. She was worried when I went to school there that I'd be—let's see—corrupted. She won't work with anyone who doesn't want her."

Sue was listening attentively. "I think my father would love to meet her. He'd be very interested in her role in the village."

"Well, then, we should see what we can arrange." Jeff turned. "Our town isn't very big." He smiled as he pointed out the functions of a few small buildings, then turned to Sue. "It's time to dance."

Sue smiled. "I'll give it a try. What do I do?"

"Just listen. The music will tell you what to do, especially the drums." They walked to the edge of the gyrating crowd and started to move.

At first Sue felt a little stiff, then started to feel the music in her body. He was right! The drums told her what to do! She was truly dancing to welcome in spring and all its wonders.

Jeff introduced his mother, Malinda, to Sue, then Sue invited her to come up the hill and meet her father. She consented to go. They chatted politely, and Sue picked up some hesitancy in Malinda's tone. "I doubt if he'll be interested in what I do," she stated before they went into the den to meet David.

After the formalities, Sue and Jeff left the room. "Let's take a walk," suggested Jeff. "Not too far," responded Sue. "They might not spend much time together."

Sue was wrong. Malinda came out of the room smiling. "He's wonderful! He knows almost as much about our culture and beliefs as I do! It is a special delight to meet someone so knowledgeable." Then her face dropped. "He is very, very ill. He wants me to work with him, but it is—almost—too late. We have agreed I will move in here and be in charge of his life for a period of time." She looked at Sue. "He is very proud of you, Sue. He said you would help in any way I choose. This must seem very strange to you, I know. I will do all the cooking." She turned to Jeff. "Sue will need help with the shopping. I want you to help her, teach her where she must go for the ingredients I need."

Sue was a little startled. "He really wants you to be that involved?"

"Yes. He wants to participate 100%. He knows he is on the edge of leaving life. He wants to try working with me. He said it will be a learning adventure for him."

Sue thought of her father's many trips and his excitement when he would find and understand new customs and beliefs. She also really felt he might only have a couple of weeks left, and wondered if she wanted a strange person intruding on what she felt was their remaining time together.

"Do you use some kind of medicine with what you do?"

"Food is my medicine. Change does not happen quickly. My concern is our time is short. Sue, don't worry about my getting in your way for you two to be together. I'll share what I'm doing as much as you want. I didn't anticipate I would look forward to working and being with him. He is a delight. If you'll excuse me for now, I have an elders meeting to attend. Jeff, you know the basics of what I'll need to start. I'll be back early enough to start supper."

CHAPTER TWO

THE NEXT STEP

The next two weeks were uneventful. Malinda created simple and tasty meals, and would often spend time chatting with David, both seeming to enjoy their encounters. Sue hardly noticed they had no meat or dairy products, since the meals were tasty and filling. David, however, was complaining that he was missing his Sunday pot roast. "Old habits can be hard to break," was Malinda's response, and they both would laugh.

David shared the letter he received from his old friend, Cal. He had inquired about David's health and wondered if he could visit at the end of the college summer semester. It would be more than three months away, and would be the first chance he would have.

David was enthusiastic and wrote a detailed letter to Cal, telling him about Malinda. He thought the three of them would have a great time sharing together and said he looked forward to a visit.

Sue was pleased her father didn't seem to be deteriorating as he had been, but also didn't seem to be improving either.

She mentioned this to Jeff who smiled and said, "He's not strong enough for rituals yet."

"Rituals? What rituals?"

"It is what my mother does. She first assesses the situation and treats her client with appropriate food. In your father's shape he will take some time to get strong enough, if he gets stronger at all. He must be strong enough to go through the rituals, based on ridding him of the demons in his body that feed on his health."

Sue blinked. It never crossed her mind that Malinda was just starting a longer process. "What will he do in a ritual?" There was a hint of fear in her voice.

"It's always different, depending on the person she's working with. It's not unusual that they may go into a trance together at first, so she can help him in the spirit world to exorcise the different demons. Occasionally, there may be one that the client must get rid of by himself. Once the cleansing is done, with the right foods, he will heal quickly."

Sue looked at Jeff. He had spoken to her as if he were describing the directions of cutting up a piece of fruit. No surprise, no hesitancy, just as if this were an everyday event.

"Does my father know this?"

"Of course. They talked about it the first day they met. Can't you tell how excited your father seems to be, looking forward to the process?" Jeff was puzzled at Sue's responses.

Then Sue realized she had been distracted by Jeff, her newest focus. She was missing a lot of new things in her father's life. "Well, he knows, and if he's happy I guess that's what counts."

CHAPTER THREE

....

THE INSTRUCTIONS

I t was three and a half months later when Cal arrived. "I can't believe how healthy you look! How much weight have you lost?"

"Oh—about twenty-five pounds."

"Is the weight loss on purpose?" asked Cal, curiously.

"Yes," smiled David. "And I've been able to walk more without pain. We've been taking the golf cart to avoid the hill. We have been walking around the square in town, gradually increasing the distance. I'm feeling stronger and healthier."

"Sue says you're going to do some kind of local ritual designed to allow you to heal even faster. Is that true? She also said there was a risk involved, and you have to be healthy enough to endure it."

"That's all true. This past month Malinda has been teaching me what I have to do. The first part can be stressful on the body. The second part's challenge is I can get <u>so</u> relaxed my heart may beat too slowly to maintain my body. We have been practicing segments of the first phase, and as I've gotten stronger my tolerance for the trip has gotten much greater. You, Sue, and Jeff can help with the second part.

When we descend, time will pass very quickly for us and we will be unaware of the length of time we have visited. It will be dangerous if we stay much more than two hours. If we do, we might not be able to return. We will need guidance back. There will be a signal system you can send that will tell us it's time to return and direct us onto the returning path." David was smiling. It was obvious he was looking forward to his adventure.

The next week went quickly for Cal and David, reminiscing about their former activities and accomplishments together. Malinda, David, and Cal were walking in the square when Malinda announced that they could make their trip the next day if David wanted.

"If I want? Of course! We can do it while Cal is still here! I'm really excited."

Malinda just smiled. She knew David knew the risks and was as ready as possible.

CHAPTER FOUR

THE TRIP

J eff, Cal, and Susan were in the den. Malinda had an old tape player there with the speakers placed in the next room.

Malinda gave them the final instructions. "When you push this button, we'll be in the next room. The player will play the sound of a drum beating. After two hours, push this button. The drum beat will stop. Then push this red button. Another drum beat will be heard, with the beat being twice as fast as the original. The drum beat tells us it's time to go, and also guide us. Without the beat, we would have no way of knowing how to come back. Do not try to awaken us. We will appear to be in a coma, or unconscious, which we will be. A part of us will be elsewhere."

She turned toward David, and put a necklace around his neck, holding a small black rock.

Jeff looked surprised. "Is that . . ."

"Yes, it's the one your father gave me many years ago before he died."

"Well, we're off. Two hours. Red button."

They walked into the room with the speakers and closed the door. Malinda called through the door. "OK. We're in our recliners. Push the first button.

Jeff leaned over and pushed the button. All was quiet except the Boom—Boom—Boom—of a slow drum beat.

David and Malinda sang their mantra and did their special breathing. It wasn't long when David felt himself get light and seemed to float out of himself. He saw Malinda and reached out to her and held hands. They started to move, with the drumbeats making a path. They went faster and faster—lights whizzing by, then darkness, the drumbeats marking the way. They slowed, then stopped in front of a large opening, like an entrance to a cave and walked in, still holding hands.

In front of them were rows of stalls as far as they could see, each with animals in them. Cows, chickens, pigs, sheep and goats. There was water with all kinds of fish, shell fish, shrimp, crabs, and scallops. Malinda had told him what to expect, yet he was surprised at what he saw. "I didn't think there would be this much," whispered David.

You've eaten many forms of life in the past. Plants don't count. These are the spirits of the life forms you've eaten, and now they live with you, eating your life force. You must be ready to let them go with a commitment you will not eat them again, or they may come back, eating triple of the life force they do now.

David heard a laugh. He turned. "Dee Dee! Am I putting myself in jeopardy?" Dee Dee laughed again, then asked, "Are you ready to give up Saturday Night roast beef and dairy, like cheese and your favorite, ice cream?"

"Who—what are you?" asked a startled Malinda.

David said, "I guess I should introduce you. Malinda, this is Dee Dee, my death angel."

Dee Dee interrupted, seeming surprised "How do you see me?"

Malinda responded, "I have allowed myself to become a part of him. It is the him in me that sees you."

Dee Dee nodded, then stated, "Time is passing."

"Yes," Malinda turned to David. "Release them." David waved his arm the way he was instructed. "I'm sorry. I didn't know. You are now released!"

Malinda reached into a stall and grabbed a piece of David's life force. It emitted a low glow. She pulled it and pushed it under David's left rib. She massaged the life force until it changed direction.

"That reconnects your life force so it can now return to you, a little at a time. The drumbeat has stopped. Time to go!"

"I'd like him to go with you," said Dee Dee. "Maybe he won't."

At the house, Jeff kept pushing the red button, but nothing happened. Cal looked over the old machinery and couldn't figure why it wasn't playing. Sue just sat and covered her eyes, murmuring, "They'll be in a coma forever," she whispered.

Jeff ran into the kitchen and grabbed the large soup pot. He went into the room with the speakers and started drumming on the bottom of the pot. It was an even, rapid beat. They all looked at each other. Cal visibly crossed his fingers for good luck.

- - - - - - - - - -

"I hear something. This way, this way."

Dee Dee pointed, "Go there." It was a different direction. "Come," whispered David to Malinda. She hesitated, then moved in the direction Dee Dee pointed. "There's the path!" she exclaimed.

The path was bumpy, but lit. They buzzed through the blurred light, slowed, then floated down to their bodies back at the house.

CHAPTER FIVE

TRADITION

The next week Jeff, David and Cal were reviewing what had happened. "If it hadn't been for Jeff's action, you wouldn't be here. Is that right?" Cal wanted to hear more from David. David nodded.

"Also, there is always meat energy left in the body if you eat living things, and their residue feeds on your life force, a little at a time, and can grow bigger in your body, replacing healthy tissue. I have pledged to eat no meat or dairy products. It hasn't been hard with Malinda's cooking."

Jeff spoke up. "Are you sure my mother said she was a part of you?"

"Yes. That's how she could see Dee Dee."

"I was surprised when she gave you that necklace. It is very special to her. In our culture it is seen like an engagement gift."

"Really? Jeff, what would you think if I asked your mother to marry me?"

Jeff was quiet for a moment, then spoke. "I think that would make her very happy. I've never seen her like this since my father died. There seems to be a new aliveness about her. And I have a question for you. What would you think if I asked Sue to marry me?"

"I'd be glad to have you as part of my family. I'm not sure how she'll answer, Jeff. She's been talking about going back to the States, now that I'm doing better. I think she is a little bored here except for the times she's with you."

David turned to Cal. "I want to be ready with a ring. Will you get me something when you go back to the states? There doesn't seem to be a jewelry store around here."

"Sure," responded Cal. "What did you have in mind?"

"Well, a diamond is pretty traditional, as long as it's a little unique, expressing my creative self. She likes the color blue. I thought maybe a sapphire—or a combination might be nice."

Jeff spoke up. "She wouldn't accept a diamond or a sapphire. In your country, the bigger the stone the better. Those with wealth often choose the biggest ring they can find, believing its value and size somehow expresses the size of their love. Does that mean people with limited resources love less? I don't think so. Here, we give something that is abundant and common to the area, available to all. It is chosen with and given in love."

"So that plain stone she gave me is more precious than any diamond or sapphire?" asked David.

"Exactly! You must choose carefully. We have an abundance of crystal, black volcanic rock and a very hard, dark wood. Any of these would be acceptable. If you like, I will take you to areas you may find something interesting to you. I will be hunting also. If Susan doesn't accept my token—well—I will know her choice."

"Could we go 'hunting' as you say, tomorrow, after we see Cal off in the morning?" David was intrigued—another new custom.

Jeff nodded. "We can talk about details along the way."

CHAPTER SIX

HUNTING

It had been an emotional parting. Cal had felt close to the people he met and was especially appreciative of his re-connection with David and Sue.

It was later, when traveling with David, that Jeff spoke of Cal. "I wish I had had more people like him as professors when I attended college. Being with him was a pleasant experience, and he never freaked out about what you and Mom were doing, just seemed to be enjoying being a part of it."

David nodded. "In truth, Jeff, Cal and I did many things together that others might have thought of as <u>strange</u>. Tell me more about what we're to do?"

"Well, we choose a point along here to stop. We relax a little, take a dozen or so deep breaths, and focus on your objective, to find an object for your person of focus that will express your special feelings. Sometimes objects are combined, but mostly they are single pieces. Then we work them at our leisure until you feel it is ready. That's it!

Start focusing," continued Jeff, as he slowed their vehicle down. After a short period of time, he stopped. "I feel some strong energy here. How about you?"

"If you mean a tingly feeling all down my arms, then this is a good place for me also." They did the breathing and focusing.

Jeff smiled as he helped David step out. They walked slowly off the main road. Jeff pointed out the things that qualified. Suddenly, David stopped. "Look! Tiny pieces of crystal." David bent over and pushed the tiny crumbles around with his fingers. A couple of small pieces seemed to be giving off a hint of blue light. David was ecstatic. "These two pieces are perfect!" He took a small box from his pocket and put the two stones in it.

"How are you doing?" "Nothing yet. Are you finished?"

"No. They are just right for something, though."

They kept wandering around the area. Jeff made a little noise. He bent over and picked up a piece of twisted black stone. The shape was very different. He toyed with the stone, moved it back and forth, hand to hand, then said, "I've found a stone for Susan." He was grinning broadly.

David was entering the area where the dark wood grew. He seemed to be attracted to a grove where some branches were broken. Near the root at the base of the tree was a flat piece of wood. David picked it up. It's so smooth," he said. "It almost feels as if it's been polished, just for me."

They both laughed. "Is that it?" asked Jeff.

"I'm sure of it," replied David. The two happy men retraced their steps back to the vehicle.

CHAPTER SEVEN

A CHANGED LIFE

It had been three weeks since Jeff had brought David the special tools to work the wood. David was pleased with the result. On the face of the diamond-shaped wood was a curved line from near the top to near the bottom. At each end of the line were the tiny stones that sometimes reflected blue.

At the top tip of the teardrop was a hole, a round piece of metal through it so a chain could go through it, leaving the curved surface to show.

David carefully wrapped a piece of cloth around it and was fidgety as he waited for Malinda to make her daily appearance.

He rushed to the door when he heard her arrive. He opened his arms and pulled her to him as soon as she crossed the threshold. "What's got you so excited," she asked—a twinkle in her eye.

"Here, sit down. I have something important to ask you."

Malinda sat down, amused at David's behavior.

He pulled out a chair and sat facing her. David started, "When we were with Dee Dee, you said you were part of me. Jeff told me how important the rock you gave me is to you. Now, this can't be a one-way thing. I have something for you—with a wish that we will be part of each other, even if my time is short."

He unwrapped his gift. "See this diamond shape? And see how this curved line brings us both together, sharing the same space—the bluish stone representing each of us. And what makes this diamond precious—it contains us both—together, in one space. You know how ill I am. Will you be willing to spend what time I have—with me?"

He stopped and looked into her eyes. Her eyes were wet and started dripping tears. At the same time, they both leaned forward and hugged each other, then stood up and continued to hug.

"You've changed my life, more than I ever dared to hope." He was whispering softly.

Malinda whispered, "I, too, am different. Together, something new happened. Yes. Yes. I want us to be together as much as possible. I love your diamond. It is filled with our love. I feel its beauty—thank you.

Susan was happy for her father and Malinda. David told her about the symbolism, and Sue just smiled. She was aware her father was happier than she had seen him in years. He also was able to move more, without pain. He acted as if he had lived here his entire life.

There was a knock at the door. Jeff seemed excited. "My mother is going to propose your father for membership in the elders' council."

Sue was puzzled. "Is that important? He is an elder."

"Oh, it's very different. If they accept the proposal, he will be interviewed by the elders. If they invite him to join, he will get a vote on the council or they may also invite him to attend as a special guest or just not allow him to attend except for public meetings." He looked at Susan. She still looked puzzled. "If he gets to vote, he will be considered one of the town's fathers. This is almost unheard of for an outsider, especially someone from the states. The town fathers own all our resources. There is no independent ownership. If someone needs something, they provide it. They funded my expenses to study in the United States."

Susan was stunned. The entire place functioned as a collaborative. She needed to know more, and Jeff was an informed and energetic teacher.

CHAPTER EIGHT

....

THE VOTE

The proposal went well. The group was impressed by Malinda's story of their descent, especially the part where Dee Dee pointed the way. They made an assumption that Death saw a task for him to complete with their community.

An arrangement was made to have an interview. Malinda briefed David. "You will be in a light. The room will be darkened. You will be asked questions, mainly about yourself. Just be you. Answer from your heart. Remember, nothing will seem strange, so share your deepest thoughts."

She gave him a brief peck on the cheek and guided him to a spotlight-lit podium next to a stool. Malinda then disappeared into the darkness.

The first questions were background questions, accomplishments, and his personal history. Then the questions changed tone.

"What matters most for you to preserve?"

"In the here and now, at least for the moment, it is to preserve my life force—my essential essence. I have some things I would like to experience, accomplish, and explore before I change form. My friend, Dee Dee, warns me when I am at risk and my behavior is beckoning her to visit. Sometimes I hurry too much for my heart to keep up with the rest of me, and she will create a little reminder for me to slow down, like a pain in my chest.

Dee Dee is my name for death, who I see as a beautiful woman. She has a quirky sense of humor. We have had a few conversations, some of which I've written about. If you'd like, I will share them with you sometime."

"What is the period of life most significant to you?"

"In some way, it is now, this moment—this moment—whoops!—I'll never see it again." He smiled.

"What have been the most stressful, least rewarding times in your life?"

"I don't know. Stress is a learning tool for me—teaching—challenging me to explore—to discover—so it is always rewarding—even if it is immobilizing in the present moment. If I choose, it can be rewarding."

"What have been activities most productive, most fulfilling for you?"

"The old cliché—is yet to come. I have had peak experiences when I catalyzed someone out of numbness into aliveness—sleep to awakeness—including myself. These times are unpredictable."

"What are 3 to 5 actions you feel define how you see yourself today?"

"How I see myself today changes moment by moment. I have a lot of ought and should examples, like birth of my child, working my way through college against the odds, but they were experiences along the way.

There are moments that have defined me—a touch at the right time, a well timed comment, a completion, a smile, a gift of pleasure.

The giver is the angel of the moment, influencing me, changing me. Then, absorbed into me, making me one with the experience."

"What is a recurring theme that comes up for you?"

"The absence of compassion is the theft of humanness."

"What has given you a lot, yet extracted too much?"

"Like Esau, selling his birthright for a bowl of porridge? I've made bad bargains, lots of them, and yet, they were my choice. If I made a bad bargain, that just demonstrated that the other side was a better negotiator than I was, and it identified an area where I needed to focus if I wanted to improve."

"What have been some tangibles that have influenced you?"

"Many people have given me nothing tangible and have influenced me a lot, if you say that hope, encouragement, knowledge, perceptions, and points of view are not tangible. I think they are tangible, though not solid objects. I can feel them, like a cool breeze on a hot day."

"What do you find humorous?"

"Seeing, hearing and getting the great cosmic jokes that are in the energy of the life force."

"What about reverence?"

"Where is it? Someone's reverence may be someone else's cosmic joke."

"What is a lingering spot of uneasiness for you?"

"When does my sun set? I'm never sure when I'll be beckoned."

It was quiet for a moment.

"You've traveled to many parts of our world, attempted to understand many cultures. Is there anything you've seen, heard, or sensed that you would have us know?"

David paused. He thought of Malinda saying, "Speak from your heart. Remember, nothing will seem strange, so share your deepest thoughts."

David squared his shoulders, then spoke.

"The mist of the unknown clouds our view. We must be vigilant, because there are demons among us, in disguise, posing, dressing, talking the right language, yet, when scratched, no compassion leaks out. These creatures are void of compassion, and without it, they are a mutant among our species.

It seems they are growing, multiplying in numbers, yet it is difficult to tell. Sometimes we can tell by their reaction to deeds of kindness. They recoil in horror when surprised by warm acts, then cover their reaction with rational statements to keep us from seeing through their disguise.

Groups who are farming love are sometimes given a type of support that ends up to be a form of sabotage if the farmers aren't diligent.

It is strange for anyone with even small amounts of compassion to understand the demon's behavior. Oh, there are often rewards of gold for that group to collect, but the route taken seems void of any awareness or care—of the consequences, wrecked lives, untreated illness, damage to children, and many spinoffs that contaminate our water, air, and our human raw material. Compassion is powerful and aids its users with special vision, insight, and energy. It is the fertilizer of hope and joy of other's growth, creating a bountiful harvest."

He had more to share, but David felt done. He stood quietly for a moment, when a voice said, "Thank you, David. You may wait outside the hall. We will call you and share our decision."

Malinda appeared, and guided David to the outside hall. She was quiet, looked at him, then said, "I must return," and left.

David felt strange. It seemed to matter if he could vote with the group, but he wanted to be able to take part in their discussions. Then he started to think of Cal. Cal would love it here. He knew that Cal felt as much at home as he did.

He and Cal had visited many places together, but this was the first one that seemed like coming home. He wondered if Cal might come and stay, maybe teaching courses by arrangement, and just finish their life here together.

He was startled when he heard Malinda call his name. He stood and joined Malinda.

The room was lit. He walked to the podium and was joined by a man who reached out and shook his hand.

Everything went quiet. The man looked directly in David's eyes and said, "Welcome, our newest voting member of the council." His smile was a seal of approval.

There was a warm applause. Then the man spoke again. "Sometimes when a new person joins us, he or she may get—well—full of themselves. If you start becoming aware of this, stay alert. You will get a message to remind you of the finiteness of our wisdom. We all have experienced come-downs." There were snickers of recognition from the audience. "We often share our learnings with each other. Again—Welcome!"

CHAPTER NINE

....

REALITY

J eff was ready. The walk in the moonlight had set the mood. Jeff put his hand in his pocket and fingered his gift just as they sat down on the porch.

"Sue, I have something special for you. I've been saving it for a special moment, and I guess this is as good as any.

This is my gift, chosen just for you." Jeff smiled, glad he was at last sharing his token with Sue.

Sue looked at the twisted rock and rolled it between her fingers. "Does this mean what I think it does—that you want to be committed to me—maybe—marry?"

Jeff nodded, smiling.

"Oh, Jeff, if it wasn't for you, I don't know what I would have done with myself in this God-forsaken place. You are—very special to me. I love being with you. Your gentleness, your caring, your thoughtfulness and respect. In a different environment I would jump at the chance to be with you."

"You mean, like the United States? I can go back there. I was thinking of returning to study alternative energy anyway. We could be together there!"

"Jeff, we live in two different worlds. My father and his friend Cal have been looking for this place all their lives. I haven't. I like the hustle and bustle of a city."

"We could be in a city. You choose. Anywhere you like!"

"That's not what I mean, Jeff. Our worlds are too far apart. Jeff, don't you notice my diamond earrings and necklace? I love expensive jewelry. I love to dress up and go to a club.

Oh, Jeff, I love owning my own house. I like a fancy car. I love to try different foods cooked by famous chefs—foods that are made from cheeses and dead animals. No, Jeff, I will not marry you. I've already decided to leave soon. Dad no longer needs me the same way he did before. And—I do love you."

The silence hung heavy in the moonlight. Then Sue spoke again, softly.

"Oh, Jeff, this is the nicest, most thoughtful gift I ever received. I will keep it always. It will remind me of your love and gentleness." Sue took out one of her earrings.

Jeff, I want you to take this diamond—from me, a gift from my world to you."

They hugged, and listened to the noisy stillness of the night.

Chapter Ten

A Tough Question

David knew he was old now, very old, and yet his mind was alert—full of knowledge and experiences. His eyes twinkle when someone takes the time to engage him in a conversation. He was not ready, though, for the questions from the eight-year-old girl.

"Where does it all go?"

"What do you mean—it?"

"You know. Stuff you learned. You studied a lot, taught at college, learned to play a piano, stuff like that. Where did it go?"

"UH—I think I still have IT," he smiled.

"Mnnn . . . Yah. But like Nanna when she was in the nursing home. She had lots of friends who knew lots of things. Lots of those people died. Where did all the things they learned go?"

"Mnnn . . . . good question." He paused—eyes up to his upper right. Mmm . . . where did they go?

YAH—*you know*. Some people work hard to learn new things—and to learn more and more. You're old and you keep reading, about lots of stuff. So where does all the learning go? I know old people die, like my Nanna did. When you die, what happens to all the stuff you've learned?"

Her big brown eyes were opened very wide, looking directly at him. Her head was tipped a little to the left, her dark hair dangling over her right cheek and chin.

David stared at her. He was taken back by her perception of his soon to come demonstration of finiteness, as well as the question itself.

"Hmmm . . . where does it go??" he murmured.

He thought of his own strivings, his dilemmas, his most challenging accomplishments and the unique ways he had learned to challenge problems. "Where does it go, indeed?" This time a mumble.

"Does all that stuff get loose in the air when someone dies? Does it float around and other people breathe it in?

I don't think so," she answered herself. "Or people would like to hang around people who are going to die so they could get smart. I don't think people do that. Lots of time, people just cry a lot, like they did when Nanna died."

And Nanna was very special—NICE!"

The girl's eyes glazed . . . remembering. "No one was as nice as she was. And after she died, nobody seemed to get any nicer—like they could get it when Nanna died. One person I know even got more nasty when she wasn't around any more."

"Sorry I couldn't help you more," he smiled. "And I want to thank you, for reminding me I don't have all the answers."